Sing

Olivia Cliff

Contents

Chapter 1 Left

"Goodbye, Bella" he said in the same quiet, peaceful voice. He leans in and plants a final kiss on my forehead. I feel it reverberate all the way to my toes, giving me an all too familiar shiver. His lips felt more similar in temperature to my skin, which the cold air of forks had taken it's affects to. I catch myself leaning into his kiss and within seconds his lips disappeared. I stumbled forward and my eyes open in shock as I now stand alone in the forest not far down the trail from my house. The trees surrounding me feel like they have grown even bigger, towering over my small frame. I wrap my arms around my torso as I search the forest for any trace of Edward. I shiver as the cold wind whips my skin. I fall to my knees as his words sink in.

He left me...

I crumble to the floor and get into foetal position as it feels like my insides begin to crumble. I feel the tears streak my face before I can control them, my arms tighten around my torso until they are clawing at the skin below the thin material. I try desperately to hold myself together, hoping that this was all some sick dream and I would wake up in Edward's arms at any given moment. I lay there for what felt like hours as the sun started to hide behind the horizon and the cold became unbearable. I lay and ponder, what I ever did to deserve such hurt. It felt like a piece of my heart had been taken away and a huge gaping hole had taken it's place, lodged deep into my chest cavity. The cold has caused me to shiver uncontrollably now and it had gotten to be pitch black, the trees around me being barely visible now. As the cold caused me to drift off, I had one final thought...

I am so pathetic for letting anyone cause me to hurt in this way...

I wake up as I feel two strong arms lift me up from the ground. I groan as I fight my heavy eyelids in a battle I am not sure that I would win. Whoever was carrying me felt super warm and I snuggle closer as I shiver from the cold. That was when my eyes open and all I can see is tan before I lose the battle and let my eyes drift shut again.

"I've got her Charlie" My eyes snap open again as I hear my father's name. Charlie!!! He must be worried sick right now. Dinner was meant to be on ages ago. I hear as footsteps run in my direction and look over grugishly as my father and Jacob run over to me with panicked and concerned faces.

"Jacob?" I grumble. I clear my throat as my eyebrows furrow "What are you doing here?"

"Here give her to me" I hear Charlie demand from whoever was holding me.

"I've got it Charlie" Jacob steps up and shares an intense look with the person carrying me. He grabs me tight as he juggles me into his arms.

"I'm okay, put me down" I groan at the jostling.

"It's okay Bella, I got you" Jacob says as he adjust me in his arms.

"I am fine, put me down Jacob" When I give him an insistent look, he glances to Charlie that doesn't look convinced but nods anyway. He gently sets me to my feet and I feel my muscles scream in protest. I lock my knees in place, determined to not let my weakness show.

"Where was she?" Charlie asked the boy behind me. I just now get a good look at him and notice how tall he is. He stands high at about 6'6" with tan skin and I recognise him from the trip to La Push beach a while back.

"Just off the trail, not too far from the house" He answers Charlie standing tall. He nods to the man behind Charlie who I recognise as Harry Clearwater before he jogs off to stand with a few other boys that look like him.

"Jesus Bells! What were you thinking wondering into the woods? Did you wanna get yourself killed?" Charlie exclaimed as he assessed me for injuries. I grab my torso and shiver, leaning against Jacob for support. He placed his arm around me and rubs my arm in an attempt to warm me up. As I think back to the reason I was in the woods, it all comes back to me and I force myself to swallow the tears. Not here, not now....

"I went for a walk with Ed-" I try to say and recognition paints Charlie's face as it clicks in. He must know the Cullen's have left town. He steps forward and takes my other side.

"I got her Jacob, can you wrap it up here. Let everyone know that I owe them all one and I am forever thankful for their help" Jacob nods and gives me one final glance before he slides his hand off my waist. Charlie and I make our way into the house, me leaning heavily on him for support. I had shivered so hard that my muscles were cramping. As we walked passed all the people who came to help, I couldn't help but feel ashamed to have caused such a panic. All this because of a boy. My cheeks flushed as I hurried to get to the door with Charlie.

When we got inside, Charlie immediately rushed me over to the couch and wrapped me in a blanket. He cranked up the heating and grabbed the second blanket from his recliner, wrapping me up tight. He disappeared into the kitchen and returned with a glass of water with some Panadol and what looked to be some toast. He stood black watching as I gulped down the water and slowly picked away at the toast, taking the pills in hopes to help with the body aches. Feeling slightly uncomfortable at his staring I placed the finished plate and cup on the coffee table and slowly rise to my feet.

"I'm okay Dad, I swear. Go and thank everyone for their help. I am just gonna shower and get ready for bed" I tried to reassure him. All I wanted to do was curl up in to bed and drown in my misery in private, his watchful eyes were not gonna be any help with that.

"Are you sure Bells? I can get you some more water" He went to reach for the cup, making an excuse to stay and try to be helpful. I snatched it up before he can reach it and hold it in between my two hands.

"I'll grab it, go. Before everyone leaves" I shoo him out the door with a wave of a hand. He reluctantly leaves through the front door and I sneak a glance to see that there is still a few people mulling around out there, packing up and getting ready to go home for the night.

I go into the kitchen and fill up my glass, leaning against the bench as I sip this one a lot slower than I did the first one. I jump as I hear the telephone dial shrill and set my glass aside. I grab the phone off the hook and press answer, bringing it to my ear.

"Swan residence, Bella speaking" I answer in case it was Charlie's work or a friend of his.

"Bella?" I hear a shocked voice on the other side of the phone "Sorry - It's Angela. I was just ringing to check if you were alright? I heard the news about the Cullen's leaving town and that no one could find you..."

I cringe as the tears burn my eyes, I blink rapidly as I clear my throat.

"Yeah, I just got lost. I took a walk in the forest, you know how my sense of direction is" I try to play it off as I feel embarrassed. School on Monday is going to be a nightmare, the whole town must know.

"I am so glad to hear you're okay, um... My mother wanted to ask if you wanted company tonight? I know you probably want to be alone right now but I - we thought you might enjoy having someone there to distract you and maybe tomorrow we could go shopping?" Angela suggested in a quiet voice, not really sure of herself.

"Sure, I would love that. I um... I really don't want to be alone tonight. Is it okay if I come and get you? I could really use an escape for a bit" I ask her as I grab onto the roots of my hair mulling it through. I really want to be alone right now but I know that if I let myself mull on it too long I will just end up breaking down and I really don't want to scare Charlie even more than I already have tonight and maybe if I have Angela over I can avoid the millions of questions and lectures he has in store for me.

"Of course, I will pack my bag now and wait out front. Do you remember where I live?" She asks as she seems to chipper up at my answer.

"Yeah of course, I will be over in 20-30 mins after a shower" I say as I see Charlie re-enter the kitchen. I give him as best a smile I could manage at this moment.

"I will wait by the door, see ya Bella"

"Bye, Ange"

Charlie takes a seat at the table and raises an eyebrow expecting an explanation. I leant against the counter facing him, taking a sip of my water.

"Why was Angela Webber calling?" He asks as he starts to untie his boots.

"She heard the Cullens left and wanted to know if I wanted company tonight" I say nonchalantly.

"Well that's nice of her" He states with a tilt of his head. I nod absentmindedly in agreement.

"I am going to pick her up after I have a shower" I add.

"Are you sure Bells? I thought you would want to go straight to bed tonight" He presses with concern.

"I think distraction is good, I don't really want to think about..."

"Because then it will feel real?" He presses tentatively with understanding on his face. I look down, determined not to let my weakness show. The tears pricked my eyes but I swallowed harshly, batting them away. I take in a sharp intake of breathe, feeling like the air stings my lungs. I take a sip of my water to keep all the feelings down.

"Exactly" I say in a small voice. He nods and doesn't press the matter further. I have never had more appreciation for Charlie than I did in that moment.

"I will be in the Lounge Room if you need me Bells" Charlie says as he makes his way out of the room. He pauses in the doorway and turns back "One more thing, please don't ever go out into the woods alone again"

I nod as he leaves the room and makes his way to the baseball game sure to be on the TV already. His words strike me and I shake my head to dispel the thoughts...

I wasn't alone, at least not until he....

****

I grab my keys off the rack after one of the most amazing showers I have had in my entire life. My muscles felt a thousand times better, the hot water melted the knots with each water drop that belted against my skin. I put on the coat hanging by the front door and shut the door behind me as I take the steps in big strides. I swing into the cab of my truck and it roars to life with a turn of the key. I jump as the radio starts to play. I cringe at the new stereo, just another reminder that this is real. I reach over to turn it off but I realise what song is playing and freeze.

"I used to bite my tongue and hold my breath

Scared to rock the boat and make a mess"

I sit and listen as I recognise the song, Katy Perry. This was one of her favourite songs... I shiver as Alice's face flashes into my head. I get a flashback of her singing along in her melodious voice as we drove to Jacksonville. I start to sing along as I feel a singular tear escape.

"So I sat quietly, agreed politely

I guess that I forgot I had a choice

I let you push me past the breaking point

I stood for nothing, so I fell for everything

You held me down, but I got up (HEY!)

Already brushing off the dust

You hear my voice, you hear that sound

Like thunder gonna shake the ground

You held me down, but I got up (HEY!)

Get ready 'cause I've had enough

I see it all, I see it now

[Chorus]

I got the eye of the tiger, a fighter, dancing through the fire

'Cause I am a champion and you're gonna hear me roar

Louder, louder than a lion

'Cause I am a champion and you're gonna hear me roar

Oh oh oh oh oh oh x3

You're gonna hear me roar

Now I'm floating like a butterfly

Stinging like a bee I earned my stripes

I went from zero, to my own hero

You held me down, but I got up (HEY!)

Already brushing off the dust

You hear my voice, you hear that sound

Like thunder gonna shake the ground

You held me down, but I got up (HEY!)

Get ready 'cause I've had enough

I see it all, I see it now

[Chorus]

I got the eye of the tiger, a fighter, dancing through the fire

'Cause I am a champion and you're gonna hear me roar

Louder, louder than a lion

'Cause I am a champion and you're gonna hear me roar

Oh oh oh oh oh oh x3

You're gonna hear me roar

Oh oh oh oh oh oh x2

You'll hear me roar

Oh oh oh oh oh oh

You're gonna hear me roar...

Ro-oar, ro-oar, ro-oar, ro-oar, ro-oar

I got the eye of the tiger, a fighter, dancing through the fire

'Cause I am a champion and you're gonna hear me roar

Louder, louder than a lion

'Cause I am a champion and you're gonna hear me roar

Oh oh oh oh oh oh x3

You're gonna hear me roar

Oh oh oh oh oh oh x2

You'll hear me roar

Oh oh oh oh oh oh

You're gonna hear me roar..."

By the time I finish, I realise that my cheeks were streaked with tears. I rubbed my face with the sleeve of my coat trying to erase all evidence, but I know my eyes will give me away if anyone actually looked close enough. I quickly turned the radio off and put the car into gear, trying to get to Angela's as fast as the truck would allow me. I pulled up in front of Angela's house and Angela came out running to get into the truck dodging the rain drops but with little success.

"Hey Ange" I try to make my voice as normal as possible as she sets her bags beside her on my truck's front seat.

"Hey Bella, I'm glad we can do this. I think a girl's night will be fun" She says as she pulls out face masks from her bag "My mum made me bring them"

The look on my face must have said it all because we both simultaneously start to laugh. It was a strange sensation to laugh, especially knowing that it was only a few short hours ago that... I slowly stop laughing as I put the truck in reverse and start the journey home. Angela doesn't press for conversation, much like Charlie in that department and I was grateful for it. I knew if any of my other friends were in her place, they would not have offered me the same courtesy. She reaches over and turns on the radio. I cringe looking away, trying to hide my distaste and holding back the urge to turn it back off.

And I never got past what you put me through

But it's wonderful to see that it never fazed you

Hello Mr. "Perfectly fine"

How's your heart after breakin' mine?"

Angela bops along to the new Taylor Swift song and starts to sing along quietly. I focus on the road as I try not to imagine a certain little pixie like vampire in her place. But I can't help but to pretend it is her and get carried away in the daydream. It hurts to think about her but I allow myself this moment, although thinking of her hurts a lot less than thinking of Ed-him. I sing along just like I would if it were her and basked in this moment.

"Mr. "Always at the right place at the right time, " baby

Hello Mr. "Casually cruel"

Mr. "Everything revolves around you"

I've been Miss "Misery" since your goodbye

And you're Mr. "Perfectly fine"

So dignified in your well-pressed suit

So strategized, all the eyes on you

Sashay away to your seat

It's the best seat, in the best room

Oh, he's so smug, Mr. "Always wins"

So far above me in every sense

So far above feeling anything

And it's really such a shame

It's such a shame

'Cause I was Miss "Here to stay"

Now I'm Miss "Gonna be alright someday"

And someday maybe you'll miss me

But by then, you'll be Mr. "Too late"

Goodbye Mr. "Perfectly fine"

How's your heart after breakin' mine?

Mr. "Always at the right place at the right time, " baby

Goodbye Mr. "Casually cruel"

Mr. "Everything revolves around you"

I've been Miss "Misery" for the last time

And you're Mr. "Perfectly fine"

You're perfectly fine

Mr. "Look me in the eye and told me you would never go away"

You said you'd never go away"

I sang hitting every note as well as I could, knowing that I would never do justice to the voice of the pixie I was imagining beside me. I pulled into my short drive way before looking over to Angela after realising I had just sung in front of her for the first time. I have not let anyone here my voice beside Alice, and I guess Jasper not that I can be sure he was really listening.

Angela had her mouth agape as she stared at me with unblinking eyes. I blush as I try to avoid her gaze and grab the keys from the ignition. I look up again and see that she it still shocked. Was my singing really that bad? I know I have nothing on Alice but I didn't think I was tone death.

"That was amazing!" She exclaimed loudly. I cringe back as I see a side of Angela I had never witnessed. She seemed way to excitable and overbearing, nothing like the shy quiet Angela I was so used.

"I'm not that good" I said self consciously as I pick at my nails.

"You sing like an angel!" She continues. I looked down and get out of the car with Angela following soon after me, juggling her bag.

"Thank you I guess... I've never really shared that with anyone, well except Ali-" I cut myself off when my heart stings and Angela looks at me with pity

"Well I think you sound really good. Jessica was talking about a talent show they are having at school the other day. Maybe you should put your name down"

"I couldn't go in front of the whole school and show them something that I haven't showed anyone else but you a-a-and..." I said nervously. She couldn't be serious, me... singing... audience...no...

"I think you should do it, prove to them and to yourself that you can do it. I understand if you don't want to do it but after you encouraged me to ask Eric out to prom I think I should encourage you to do the same thing" She said persuasively. I guess I did encourage her to take her shot and be brave and now it was my turn to be the brave one. Prove that I am not going to be the pathetic Bella that followed Ed-him around like a lost little puppy.

"I will help you the whole time if you need support?" She suggested. I seriously pondered her request and really tried to consider it.

....

So.... Will Bella say yes? Will she wimp out? Tell me what you think?

Please vote and comment!

Chapter 2 Ideas

Hey! I'm hoping you guys enjoy this chapter! I'm having so much fun writing this book! Thanks to everyone who reads and supports this book! I decided that I would like the actor for Angela to be different so I thought long and hard and I have decided on Nina Dobrev!

Disclaimer: I don't own twilight or any of the songs featured in this book.

Edited

Chapter 2: Ideas

I hugged her. I craved the contact of her skin, hoping that it would fill the empty void in my chest. And for a second or two it did, at least it distracted me from the pit. She took a second but reluctantly she wrapped her arms around me. I held onto her for a little while and I could tell that she knew I needed this. I am not a hugger, but right now I really didn't care. Angela patted my back and the tapping caused me to relax into her embrace. I held the tears at bay for what felt like the millionth time today. She felt safe, she felt warm, she felt human. I sigh as I reluctantly step back and let her go. She gives me a reluctant smile as she shyly tucks a strand of hair behind her ear.

"Thank you" I whisper to her with the utmost gratitude.

"Does that mean you're going to do it?" she asked trying to seem like she wasn't forcing me. I mulled over it for a second longer and knew that if I really wanted to get out of my comfort zone and put on a face that Ed-him leaving me didn't affect me at all, than I had to do it. So I answer her with the most reluctant and unenthusiastic nod that I have probably ever done in my life.

Truth be told, the talent show was conveniently occurring right at the time I needed it to. It acted like a pushing force that would make me get out of the very safeguarded comfort zone that I had become way to reliant on. Ed-He used to push me into this zone, claiming it to be the safest place for me, but with him... gone (I outwardly cringe at the word). It allows me to become my own person and truth be told, taking a step back I really despise the Bella I had become. Reliant, dependent and worst of all vulnerable and weak. I want to be independent and strong willed like I was before him. I want the confidence of Rosalie. The compassion of Carlisle. The kindness of Esme. The calmness of Jasper. The fast wit of Emmett. And most of all the optimistic view on life that my pixie like friend Alice had. I just wanted to become myself again... A better version of me, one that shows the world that his departure had no effect on me. I don't need anyone... I have myself. Growing up I relied on me, and that shouldn't of changed and I won't let it happen again.

"I'm gonna do it" I smile slightly at Angela and she breaks out in a bright smile in response, happy that she had returned the favour by encouraging me to get out of my comfort zone.

"And I will help" she said as she smiled.

"Let's get inside, shall we?" I ask as I pull the coat around me closer. The rain had stopped outside during our talk but the cool Forks air was still in full effect. I open the front door for her and allow her to walk in. I realise this is the first time she had been inside the house.

"Bells?" Charlie calls out as the door clicks close behind us.

"It's me" I call back to assure him that I am home safe.

I hear him shuffle off the couch and make his way down the hallway from the lounge room.

"Oh. Hi Angela, how have you been?" Charlie asked politely as he came into view and spotted the company beside me.

"Good and you Chief Swan?" She asked politely.

"I'm good too and call me Charlie" he replied while giving her a polite smile in response.

"Ok Charlie" she replied smiling back "Thank you for letting me stay and keep Bella company"

"Of course, anytime we would love to have you over" Charlie nodded "and thanks for helping Bells out, I really appreciate it"

"Anytime Chie- Charlie" She smiled back.

"I will be in the Lounge Room if you need me" He wanders back and as he reaches the door he turns over his shoulder "and keep it down tonight, I am on morning shift tomorrow"

"Will do, we won't be up late. Angela mentioned shopping in Seattle so we will be up nice and early to make the drive"

"In your truck?" He asks with a doubtful look.

"Yeah" I confirm with a slight nod.

"Are you sure it can make it?" He looks doubtful. I cringe, remembering him saying the same thing. It was his excuse to spend time with me, back when... I shake off the memory and shake my head at Charlie. I clear my throat and bite back the hurt.

"It will be fine dad, we will stop for fuel along the way. I won't push it too hard" Charlie still doesn't look convinced but nods anyway.

"Okay be safe, call me if you need help, okay. Night Bells. Angela" He nods to both of us before retreating to his game of Baseball.

I gesture for Angela to make her way up the stairs. She juggles her bag and I follow closely behind. We make it to my bedroom and I see that Charlie had been kind enough to get the extra mattress out and place it on the floor beside the bed. Sometimes his thoughtfulness chokes me up, I swallow the lump in my throat. Angela sets her bag down and we both get comfortable for the night. I show her where the shower is and we both get into our Pyjamas ready for sleep.

"Thank you for keeping me company Ange" I say as we settle under our covers.

"Its okay Bella, that's what friends are for"

....

So what do you think? Love it? Hate it? I have put some of the cast on the side! I have changed them all so please don't hate me for it! the cast would be pimped to look like their characters!

Please vote and comment!

Chapter 3 Shopping

Hey! Here's chapter 3! Hope you like it! The outfits they wore are in external link!

Disclaimer: I don't own twilight or any songs featured in this book.

Edited

Chapter 3: Shopping

I woke up the next morning after a restless sleep, I had tossed and turned all night. I turn slowly and notice the alarm clock was reading 6 o'clock. I got up and gently woke Angela knowing we would need to get going if we wanted to get there in time.

After we both have a quick shower, we get ready as Angela changes into the outfit she brought. She looked cosy in an oversized knitted pink sweater, rolled at the sleeve and ripped blue grey skinny jeans. She wore comfortable white sneakers, ready for a day of walking through the mall.

I browse my closet and blink in shock... Clothes (obviously)... But more than half of them aren't mine. I shuffle through some of them in confusion as I try to figure out where they came from. I spot a tiny white corner peeking out of the pocket of a pair of black ripped denim jeans and pluck the note out.

'Happy Belated Birthday Bella :) Please don't hate me :(Your clothes were a welcomed donation at the Women's shelter -Alice'

I felt the tears well but as Angela made her way towards me I blinked them back and tucked the note back into the pocket it came from. Alice must have snuck in here when Edward and I were out in the forest and set this up, she knew.... I try not to dwell on this realisation as I grab out the first sweater I can find which happened to be a primrose pink coloured turtleneck. Pink was not a colour I ever wore, for as long as I can remember I had worn very neutral toned clothing. I would on occasion wear a dark green or blue but I never strayed. But this closet popped with colour, it was quite overwhelming but I knew that it will be good for me to experiment. Actually try to understand fashion, key word being try.

I hesitate but grab for the black denim pair of jeans, housing Alice's secret note. Possibly the last trace of her I have apart from my memories. I never wear skinny jeans either, especially ripped ones, the last time was a few years back when my mother had convinced me to try some on. Alice definitely knew this and I could tell she knew that I would not be impressed with this wardrobe. But if Alice taught me anything it's that, clothes make impressions and if there was anyway to convince the world that I was as confident and independent that I want to be. Change the outside and the inside will follow. I quickly dress and go to grab shoes, again being shocked to find that a lot of them had been replaced by heels of all shapes and sizes. I cringe before grabbing a pair of black doc martin like boots that seemed to be the closest to the ground and looked the most comfortable out of them all, reminding myself to buy a pair of sneakers in our shopping trip.

After I get the boots on, Angela gives me a once over but decides not to say anything just giving me a nod and an encouraging thumbs up. We had on very similar outfits, not quite matching but to a stranger it might look like we coordinated it.Oh well. We make our way down stairs to eat breakfast, trying to grab something quick so we could get out the door. We both decided on the brown cinnamon sugar pop tarts. The moment we took the last bite of our pop tarts we raced out the door, for me it was more like cautiously fast walked as I grew accustomed to the new boots. They were a lot bulkier than my regular sneakers. I cringe slightly thinking about the heels waiting for me. Damn you Alice! We both jumped into my old rusty truck, and I sent a silent prayer to whoever was listening to bless my truck to make it to Seattle..

Last night I had decided that I was going to use the money that I had saved from working at the Newton's store and the money the Cullen's had given me for my birthday, which took a lot of bargaining for me to accept, and do what I should have done a while ago; buy a suitable car now that it seemed the truck wasn't as reliable as it was. With Ed-him driving me to school most days, it had become quite run down and though it broke my heart, I knew it needed replacing. I hadn't told Charlie my plan and knew that it would be a shock to him when I brought a new car home but I knew that messaging him now may distract him from work and thought better of giving him the heads up, after all who doesn't like a good surprise right?

....

After a long drive, we arrived in Seattle. We decided to hit the mall first and browse the car dealerships afterwards.

We pull up to Pacific Place, searching desperately to find a car park. Once I found one, I carefully park the large Chevy. It looks out of place in the busy car park and sticks out like someone wearing yellow in a crowd full of black. I pat the hood in appreciation but grimace as a shower of paint chips fall to the tarmac below.

The first place we head was the bank, I needed to know exactly how much they had transferred in to my account. As we walked to the bank I noticed that I had forgot my phone in the car.

"Shoot! I forgot my phone in the car, I'll be back in a second. Meet you at the bank" I say as I start to carefully jog to the truck.

I opened the door of the truck and grabbed my phone that lay in the middle console. I look up when I hear the clicks of cameras going off. I search the mob and see a flash of a female standing in the centre of it all. I couldn't get a good glimpse as their security guards completely surround them shielding them from the gathering crowds. The guards had started to make their way through the crowd to make a pathway towards the mall for this person. I look closer trying to see who is causing such crowds to form. I saw a glimpse before their guards had solidified the shield around them again. She had blonde hair and a tall frame but I couldn't identify her in such a short amount of time.

I decide to make my way back to Angela before she gets worried. I jog over to the bank and noticed Angela out front waiting with a little bit of worry on her face as she looked around the crowds before she spotted me and jogged to meet me halfway.

"I was just about to go looking for you, where were you?" she asked in relief.

"I got distracted there is a mob of paparazzi following someone into the mall. I tried to get a glimpse but she was pretty heavily surrounded, tall blonde. Wonder who it was" I explain to Angela why it took me a little longer. I felt a little frustrated that I couldn't get a better glimpse of her face but overly curious about the mystery woman.

"You should head in and check your account" she said as she nods her head towards the banks door. I make a start and as I enter, Angela leans against the wall outside to wait

"Okay, I'll be back in a minute" I say as I walk into the bank and she gives me a succinct nod with a friendly smile.

There was only a few people in here, lining the room. The smell of clean carpet and money filled my nostrils, which sounded odd but there is no other way to describe it. I walked up to an available counter to a profession-ally dressed lady that was busily typing away at her computer. She looks up as I approach and gives me a friendly smile.

"What can I do for you today?" she asked in a subtle southern accent. Her ginger hair fell softly in curls over her shoulder and her crystal blue eyes shined with an overly keen look, definitely the overly helpful type.

"I'm here to check the balance on my account" I request with a smile in return.

"Of course, what was your BSB and Account Number? I will need some ID as well" she replied. I told her my account details and handed her my licence. After she had confirmed my details, her eyes flashed with shock as she looks at the details on her screen. She quickly hid her shock and printed out my account balance, handing me the paper and my card back

"Thank you" I say with a polite smile as the nerves kick in and I dread to look down at the paper in my hands.

"Of course, anytime. Enjoy the rest of your day" she gives me a final smile, I nod and make my way to the exit. I get outside and take a deep breath before joining Angela to lean against the wall. I pack my card away as I work up the courage to look. Surely it won't be too bad, maybe like $100 or so, my grandma used to put $100 in my trust fund every year for my birthday. I could deal with $100, but knowing the Cullen's and their abundant lack of care when it came to money, I knew that I was deluding myself to think it would be a small amount. As I finally get the will to look, I turn the paper over and feel my eyes go wide. Suddenly the ladies reaction at the bank seemed like an understatement.

"Alice" I mutter in anger as I run a hand through my hair. I glanced for a second time at the paper and see the transaction history. There was my normal pay transactions from my work at the Newton's store, but at the very top of the sheet the final transaction stood out.

+ 13 September	$1,000,000	Al-
ice Cullen		Happy Birthday! Maybe it's
time		to get that
new car :) Put		the
rest towards college		

"Bella, what's wrong?" Angela asked with obvious concern at my reaction. I handed her the piece of paper. She looked at the paper and seemed to be in even more shock then I was which I didn't think could be possible. Alice's message rings through my head and I get suspicious that she knew this would happen. Did she know he would leave me and wanted to give me some money to live the rest of my life? Like some kind of final pay out before I retire as Ed-his girlfriend. Did she see that I would want to get a new car after and did this in preparation. It was hard to imagine that the happy, bubbly Alice that planned out my birthday party would have done so knowing it would go bad. I shake the thoughts out of my head and try not to think about it too much, knowing it will drive me insane.

"Current balance......$1,011,569!" she said in shock of the large amount of money, pulling the paper closer to her face "I knew they were rich but..."

"Alice said she transferred money but I had no idea... I have to send it back" I say in shock but I knew that I promised I would accept it without complaint but I assumed it would be much smaller. With them no longer here, I knew realistically I couldn't transfer it back. I didn't have any of the details I needed to do that, especially such a large amount. plus knowing them, they probably shut the account it came from and transferred it to a new one when they moved away. It would cause a lot of issues to try and send it back so I knew that I had keep my promise and accept it without complaint "I promised I would accept it"

"You can't send it back now, it's too late" I nod at Angela's statement with reluctance as acceptance dawns and I knew we had to start shopping so that we don't make it back to Forks too late. We both turn to walk into the closest clothing store and despite all my instincts screaming at me not to go in, that shopping is not my thing, I walk in. I hear the distinct sound of the radio in the store and the sound of people chatting casually in some of the aisles. I get overwhelmed with the amount of clothes in every corner and surface of the store. For all Alice's qualities, her ability to shop was not one I had really respected until now. I decide to start with the first aisle and just make my way through, not really sure what I was doing. I started to grab some items that I liked, clothes that I normally wouldn't pick out for myself but know that I needed to start wearing to gain confidence. I recognise the song on the radio and see that Angela has heard it too.

"I adore this song" I say to Angela a little bit louder to makes sure she could hear. The lady down the aisle from us let's out a slight giggle at my enthusiasm over the song. Her blond hair bouncing on her shoulders.

"Me too, sing with me" Angela replied with a shy wink and a laugh.

"[Verse 1:]

Loving him is like driving a new Maserati down a dead-end street

Faster than the wind, passionate as sin, ending so suddenly

Loving him is like trying to change your mind once you're already flying through the free fall

Like the colours in autumn, so bright just before they lose it all

[Chorus:]

Losing him was blue like I'd never known

Missing him was dark grey all alone

Forgetting him was like trying to know somebody you never met

But loving him was red

Loving him was red"

I started to sway a little while continue to look through the racks picking out outfits of interests. Angela was nodding her head to the music while glancing at me every few seconds in awe, she had stopped singing to herself so she could listen. I felt slightly embarrassed but with it being basically just us in this aisle, I continued.

[Verse 2:]

Touching him was like realizing all you ever wanted was right there in front of you

Memorizing him was as easy as knowing all the words to your old favourite song

Fighting with him was like trying to solve a crossword and realizing there's no right answer

Regretting him was like wishing you never found out that love could be that strong

[Chorus:]

Losing him was blue like I'd never known

Missing him was dark grey all alone

Forgetting him was like trying to know somebody you never met

But loving him was red

Oh, red

Burning red

[Bridge:]

Remembering him comes in flashbacks and echoes

Tell myself it's time now, gotta let go

But moving on from him is impossible

When I still see it all in my head

In burning red

Burning, it was red

[Chorus:]

Oh, losing him was blue like I'd never known

Missing him was dark grey all alone

Forgetting him was like trying to know somebody you never met

'Cause loving him was red

Yeah, yeah, red

We're burning red

[Post-Chorus:]

And that's why he's spinnin' 'round in my head

Comes back to me, burning red

Yeah, yeah

His love was like driving a new Maser-"

I stopped abruptly as I turn to go to the next aisle and come face to face with someone's chest. I take a step back and look up at the person I avoided a near collision with, ready to apologise for not paying attention. I freeze as her face comes into view....

The blonde just passed shoulder length hair...

The tall slim figure...

The bright red lips....

I was in total shock as my brain pieces together the person standing in front of me.

It was..........

TAYLOR SWIFT!

....

Hope you like it if you do than please vote and comment! Thank u 4 reading!

Chapter 4 Meeting Taylor

Hey readers! So this is my 4th chapter! I hope everyone enjoys this! Thanks for reading! dress she brought on the side!

Disclaimer: I don't own twilight or any songs featured in this book.

Edited

Chapter 4: Meeting Taylor

"Um... Sorry that I nearly ran into you" I say after coming back from the initial shock.

"Don't worry you were distracted. You have a beautiful voice. Have you ever thought about becoming a singer?" She asked with a polite friendly smile on her face.

"Um... Not really, I-I knew I couldn't compare to p-people as like you. N-Not that I wouldn't love to be a singer. I-I just don't think I have the confidence" I said my voice shaking slightly. I felt myself blush in embarrassment and took a deep breath hoping to pull myself together, I must look like such a wreck. But it was so forward that I couldn't help but become a little flustered.

"I think you could definitely do it with the right manager supporting you. I am sure the scouts would love to to take a listen to your demo" she says calmly and collectively, as if she did something like this all the time. I looked at Angela and she nodded encouragingly.

"I guess? But I don't really have a demo" I said nervously.

"They could come to a performance? Do you have any gigs coming up?" She asked patiently as the security guard behind her began talking into his earpiece, giving his other colleagues his whereabouts.

"Um... We have a school talent show coming up" I offer in hope as she nods and mulls it over.

"That could work. What's your name?"

"Isabella Swan, but Bella for short"

"What high school do you attend?" she asks as she gets the latest iPhone out of her pocket. I take a deep breath as it all started to feel real. Taylor Swift was asking for my name...

"I go to school at Forks High school and the talent show is on the 2nd of October at 5 o'clock" I say, trying my hardest to keep my voice calm and understandable. She nods typing away in her phone, not even a glance in my direction as her eyebrows furrowed in concentration.

"Okay, I'll be back in a second. Just going to check in with my manager and arrange a few things. Hopefully I won't be busy because I would love to come and watch" she explained before she walked out of the store, bringing her phone to her ear. I pinched myself to make sure this wasn't a dream.

"Ouch" I whispered with a flinch, rubbing my arm which now holds a small red mark. I look up, trying to will myself to believe this was real as I see

Taylor through the glass of the shop window talking on the phone with her security guards surrounding her, blocking her from sight.

I turned towards Angela who was in an equal amount of shock. I waved my hand in front of her face. She blinked once... twice.... three times before looking at me with astonishment.

"I can't believe it! You could be famous in like a months time" she exclaimed excitedly but quiet enough to make sure no one heard. She looked just as frazzled as I felt and i knew we were both questioning what was happening right now.

"That's if I make it... You have to remember the music business is tough. So don't let your hopes get too high, scouts see many people every day. I seriously think that I won't make it" I replied feeling slightly defeated but still quite excited to even get an opportunity like this.

"You will make it, I have faith in you. Your voice is better than you give yourself credit for" She encourages smiling at me. I gave her a half smile in return. Not really believing too much into her enthusiasm.

"I agree with her" I hear Taylor say gently from behind me. I turn to see her smiling friendly with an open posture as she tucks her cell phone into the front pocket of her light beige shorts. Her white blouse hang loosely, tucked in neatly allowing it to billow slightly at the bottom. Her blonde hair was down in a cute curly style with a fringe lining her heart shaped face. Her knee high boots were an exact match in shade as her shorts and helped tie her outfit together.

"Thanks" I say looking between the both of them, I was never one for taking compliments.

"So...." I continue whilst looking pointedly at Taylor, trying to fish infor-mation from her in regards to the phone call she just made and get the attention away from myself for a bit. She seemed to understand what I was hinting at and nodded.

"Oh right, well they will be sending a scout and camera man out to watch and record your performance. It also turns out that I am free that night, so... I will be able to see it live. Most likely in a disguise though" she says in slight excitement, sharing the news with us. I smile at her excitement and can't help but feel a similar amount bubble up inside of me, plus a bundle of nerves.

"Wait, what will happen if the scout thinks I'm good enough?" I ask, curious about what happens next.

"Well, the scout will send the video to numerous recording companies and see what companies respond, if any do. From there you chose which company you would like to record with, sign a few papers, audition and record a few songs to see if you can cope with the recording process and if you pass then they will let you start recording the next top hit" she explains.

"Okay, and what were you saying about a manager?" I asked her in confusion. All of this was making an absolute mess in my head. I had never looked much into the life of celebrities, never taking all that much interest so all of this was a whole new world to me.

"Oh, if you end up signing a record deal you'll need a manager to help organize your schedule like when your concerts will be held and when you will be on talk show, ect, ect. But when you first start out your manager could be a family member, a friend, just anyone that is willing to help you until you can hire professional help. My dad was my first ever manager, I remember the days he used to sell my albums in a Walmart car park" she laughs with a helpful smile on her face. I looked over at Angela who was standing behind me as the wheels start to turn. She is smart and seems to support me, calms me down and seems to be able to remain calm in situations like this.

"That's a great idea Taylor... Angela would you consider being my manager?" I asked hope filling my tone. I obviously was not putting any pressure on her as I knew this would be a big ask, especially as we were both still seniors in high school.

"I guess? It would be fun and I have always liked organising things" she said with excitement lacing her slightly nervous tone.

"I think you will be great but if you ever wanna tap out, just tell me" I give her a brief hug before we both turn back to Taylor not really sure what else needs to be said.

"Would you like to accompany me shopping? My friend was meant to join but they had a last minute audition" Taylor asked seeing the hesitation on our faces on what to say next.

"Of course, we would love too" I say back feeling slightly nervous about the fact that a celebrity wanted to spend more time in my presence. Just a few hours, just a few hours more to try and not embarrass myself in front of her. I can do this. What would Alice do? This is my new motto that I will now live vicariously through. The answer would be to shop confidently in stride with Taylor as if she belonged there, none of this nervousness and worrying over embarrassment that hasn't even happened. It wasn't even just Taylor, she had bodygaurds and fans that would be watching her every move and with me beside her... they will watch mine too.

Anxiety will not get you out of your box, you can do this Bella.

I hooked arms with Angela hoping that she wouldn't let me fall in front of everyone. She seemed to understand and gripped me slightly tighter. My clumsiness was not gonna ruin this. Taylor followed behind us as we headed towards the dressing room as we had outfits to try on. As we reached the dressing rooms we all separated going into separate stalls to try on our selections.

I tried on several outfits much to my dismay, in the end I decided I would take them all. I walked out to see Angela talking to Taylor and as I approached they both turned and smiled.

"Are we ready to pay?" I asked smiling back, tucking a stray hair strand behind my ear. I couldn't believe I was actually shopping with Taylor Swift. I'm by no means a swiftie I think they call themselves but I still loved her music.

"Yep" they replied at the same time before we all laughed.

We made our way over to the counter, there was a younger female leaning on the bench. She had delicate features that matched her small frame well. She had a soft but friendly smile as she sees us approach. I grabbed the clothes Angela was planning on buying, adding them to my pile. I smiled at her as she went to protest but I simply waved the piece of paper from the bank and she closed her mouth but still seemed to hesitate. I dumped the large pile of clothes on the counter and the clerk looked down surprised by how much I was buying. She started to scan them without another look in my direction, seemingly happy that I had gotten so much.

"So the total comes to $659.98" she said. I nodded my head before swiping my card and entering the pin, with a slight flinch that I couldn't contain. I hate spending money I didn't earn. Once it had approved Angela and I stepped aside to let Taylor pay for her clothes. The look on the clerks face when she saw Taylor was priceless Angela and I couldn't help but giggle a little, trying to keep it silent. It was too funny, but I couldn't help but to feel pity for the girl as not long ago I was her. As soon as she had also paid she grabbed her bags, gave the clerk a quick signature and a photo before making her way over to us.

"Does that happen every time?" I can't help but ask with a slight chuckle. taylor looks over her shoulder at the clerk who still seemed to be mulling over the interaction that had just occurred.

"Like 75% of the time, sometimes they don't know me or are too shy to approach" She shrugs nonchalantly "Although if I can tell it's the later, I like to approach them if I can"

"That's actually really cool" I smile at her and she seems to actually somewhat blush at the compliment. She turns to assess the front door seeming to grimace at what she saw.

"Just a heads up, the paparazzi are pretty bad today. Words gotten out that I am here. If you want to shop separately I will completely understand" she warns us, she seems a little concerned as she searches our faces for any sign of hesitancy. I could tell this has scared people off before, hence why she felt the need to warn us. I put on a smile, pretending that this doesn't completely terrify me.

"Let's do this" I look to Angela and she seems to have the same attitude that I do, giving me a determined nod. Angela and I linked arms preparing for the awaiting crowd that has brewed, I hesitate but offer my other arm to Taylor and she takes it without even really thinking about it. This way we don't lose each other in the crowd and it will be easier for security to make a path. We stepped out of the comfort of the store and flashes erupted from every direction. It dazed me for a moment as I blink a few times to adjust.

"Keep your heads down, helps with the flashes" Taylor warns us again, as we duck our heads and let her team lead us through the crowd. We used our hair to cover our faces as we watch the ground below, letting our linked arms lead us the right way. The security made a path for us to walk through and we quickly made our way towards the food court. The mall security had stepped in and had seemed to manage to keep the group at bay. Taylor stopped abruptly, I looked up in surprise to see what had captured her attention alarmed. I turned to see her looking toward a dress in the shop window we were about to walk past. It was a beautiful satin strappy red dress that came to just above knee height, it had simple structure but was still absolutely gorgeous. Taylor wordlessly started to pull us into the shop.

"Are you going to get the dress?" I asked her in confusion from the encounter.

"Not me but I think you are" she replies with a mischievous smile. My eyebrows burrow as I look at her bewildered.

"But it's so fancy, I wouldn't have anywhere to wear it to. Forks is tiny" I make a rebuttal, looking at her dazed at why she thinks I would need this dress.

"You'll wear it to the talent show, it's perfect" she suggests as she scans the store looking for the dress that we had seen on the mannequin.

"Are you sure? Isn't it a little too fancy?" I ask with doubt, allowing myself to be dragged through the store on this dress hunt that we had now become a part of.

"No, I think it's just the right amount of fancy. What size?"she replies distractedly as she file through the dress on the rack.

"Small" I replied still processing what was happening, she grabbed the right one and walked up to the counter. With us following along for the ride. I look to Angela and all we can do is raise each others eyebrows and shrug. This time we approach a young male clerk about mid twenties that seemed just as dazed as the first one. He shot upright as soon as he made eye contact with her and seemed to be slightly hyperventilating as Taylor put the dress onto the counter. After the whole interaction, I realised that she had paid for the dress. By the time I saw, it was too late to protest but when I went to open my mouth she simply held up a hand and handed me the bag.

"Consider it a gift to wish you luck and for joining me on this shopping trip. Maybe to the start of a new friendship" she explains as she gives the clerk one final wave as we exit the store.

"So we're kind of friends?" I asked, even shocked at the thought of it.

"I think we will be great friends, even if you don't end up being signed" she replies with an encouraging smile. I can't help but smile back as Angela gives my arm an encouraging squeeze. I hope she doesn't feel left out of this. I turn to look at her and see her genuinely happy face. She is such a good friend, I could tell she is the type to celebrate her friends successes as her own. I really should have spent more time with her this past year.

"Shall we make our way to the food court?" she asked with her eyebrows raised, as if asking if we are hungry.

"Yes please, I'm starving. Angela?" I answer before looking to Angela.

"Food sounds great" She smiles back. I nod and we follow Taylor's security in the direction of the food court. Some of the paparazzi had seemed to break through and had once again gathered waiting outside the food court, looking in all directions for Taylor. When they spotted us, we immediately ducked our head. Letting the security make a path for us again.

"The down side of fame besides the haters is that you can never go anywhere without paparazzi following you! No privacy at all!" Taylor muttered annoyed, as she tried to speak over the noisy clicking and numerous questions being thrown in her direction. The food court came into sight through the spaces in the crowd.

"What does every one want?" she asked loudly looking back at us as we push through.

"I really want a burger?" I asked them unsure as it would be easier to agree on one place.

"Sure!" They both responded with nods. We started to walk towards a restaurant that was kind of offsetted to the rest of the food court as Taylor whispered in one of her team members ears. As soon as we walked in the door, the security held the paparazzi at bay. When the staff saw who had entered we were seated immediately, in one mad rush. We were placed in what seemed to be what was considered the best seats they had.

"I guess that's one upside" she said with a slight giggle at our dazed looks. I laughed a little too as Angela and I shared bewildered looks. The waitress came over to take our order before we had really even had a chance to look at the menu. Now that's service.

....

Love it? hate it? tell me what you think.

Please comment and vote

Chapter 5 Karaoke

Hey guys! Here's chapter 5! hope you like it! thanks for reading!

Disclaimer: I don't own twilight or or any songs featured in this book.

Editing - This chapter is a little rough

Chapter 5- Karaoke

The restaurant smelt amazing, the aromas of garlic and freshly diced onion wafted through the space. It had a modern woody vibe with a warm atmosphere that seemed to be buzzing with the people that took up the space inside. Once we were seated comfortably, we all ordered and the waitress informed us that it was karaoke evening and handed us a booklet of songs. I could tell she was particularly keen to give Taylor a booklet. Once she was out of sight we started looking through the book, each of us finding some of our favorite songs.

"Bella you should sing, a little sneak peak performance" Taylor suggested with the utmost confidence in me. Despite only knowing me for a short time, she seemed to have adopted a lot of optimism in my singing ability, despite not even knowing the full extent to what I was capable of. I appreciated her a lot in this regard, as it was the confidence I lack and so badly want to achieve.

"Really? Are you sure?" I asked not feeling entirely competent to sing in front of a restaurant filled with people. Especially people that I now notice have their eyes glued to our table, watching our every move.

"Yes, of course. I'll go first if you want?" she replied, seeing my reluctance. I thought about her proposition for a second... Wait if she goes first, that will mean I have to compete with her because I know she will kill her performance. I mean she has sung for arenas so this restaurant will be a walk in the park. I don't wanna have to be the following act.

"No it's fine, I'll go first. It will be good to face the nerves. What should I sing though?" I questioned to myself. I browsed the list looking for a song I know that I sing and know at least moderately well, not wanting to embarrass myself. After looking through the list I decided on a song that I have sang a multitude of nights in the shower. I tried not to stumble as I made my way to the person in charge of the karaoke and instead attempted to stride, faking the confidence I definitely did not have right now. I told him that I wanted to sing 'Listen' by Beyonce. He nodded getting me to fill out a small request form with my name and song choice before handing me a mic with a smile, he gestures towards the stage with words of good luck. My first step on the stage, I felt my legs start to shake. I stop for a couple of seconds, close my eyes and just take a singular deep breath. You can do this, this is what Alice or Ed-he would have never thought you could achieve. Prove them wrong.

With a final deep breath I force myself to smile and make my way to the middle of the stage, not letting my shaking legs deter me. Taylor and Angela smiled encouragingly at me, Taylor gestured for me to look at her.

'Pretend it's only us' She mouths, and I nod before looking towards the DJ and bowing my head to begin. The opening chords started to play and I knew I had the whole restaurants attention but I only looked at my table. Locking eyes with Angela for support. I noticed Taylor was filming in my peripheral and this only made me focus harder on Angela before I ran off the stage...

"Listen to the song here in my heartA melody I start but can't completeListen to the sound from deep within It's only beginning to find release

Oh, the time has come for my dreams to be heardThey will not be pushed aside and turnedInto your own all 'cause you won'tListen

Listen, I am alone at a crossroadsI'm not at home in my own homeAnd I've tried and tried to say what's on mindYou should have known

Oh, now I'm done believing youYou don't know what I'm feelingI'm more than what you made of meI followed the voice you gave to meBut now I've gotta find my own

You should have listenedThere is someone here insideSomeone I thought had died so long ago

Oh, I'm screaming out and my dreams'll be heardThey will not be pushed aside on wordsInto your own all 'cause you won'tListen

Listen, I am alone at a crossroadsI'm not at home in my own homeAnd I've tried and tried to say what's on mindYou should have known

Oh, now I'm done believing youYou don't know what I'm feelingI'm more than what you made of meI followed the voice you gave to meBut now I've gotta find my own

I don't know where I belongBut I'll be moving onIf you don't, if you won'tListen to the song here in my heartA melody I start but I will complete

Oh, now I'm done believing youYou don't know what I'm feelingI'm more than what you made of meI followed the voice you think you gave to me

But now I've gotta find my own, my own" I finished hitting every note to the best of my ability. It was quiet for a few seconds after the song came to an end, I felt like the silence was echoing in my ears before everyone in the restaurant erupted into applause. I blush hard as I can't help but smile, I give a slight nod to the crowd before walking off and giving my microphone back to an overly happy and impressed DJ.

I made my way back to the table, getting smiles from all the tables on my way past. Taylor met me halfway, engulfing me in an airtight hug. I hugged her back with the same amount of volition.

"Incredible!" she compliments in complete awe. We then released each other noticing everyone still gawking awkwardly. I start to make my way over to the table after whispering a slightly shy 'thank you' to Taylor. Angela also wrapped me up in a tight hug when I reached our table. I took my seat and turned to see Taylor taking the microphone from a shocked DJ.

"Hello everyone. What you heard just now is my new acquaintance and a possibly upcoming star, Bella! I don't know if I can compare to that incredible performance but I will try" she boasts through the microphone and the crowd applause, glancing in my direction with an array of looks. I blush and look down as everyone's eyes seemed to assess me further, praying that Taylor would start singing soon to divert the attention. I glance up to see Taylor nod in the general direction of the DJ that still seemed to be dazed, I swear I saw him pinch himself from the corner of my eye.

"I remember when we broke up the first time

Saying, "This is it, I've had enough," 'cause like

We hadn't seen each other in a month

When you said you needed space. (What?)

Then you come around again and say

"Baby, I miss you and I swear I'm gonna change, trust me."

Remember how that lasted for a day?

I say, "I hate you," we break up, you call me, "I love you."

Ooh, we called it off again last night

But ooh, this time I'm telling you, I'm telling you

We are never ever ever getting back together,

We are never ever ever getting back together,

You go talk to your friends, talk to my friends, talk to me

But we are never ever ever ever getting back together

Like, ever...

I'm really gonna miss you picking fights

And me falling for it screaming that I'm right

And you would hide away and find your peace of mind

With some indie record that's much cooler than mine

Ooh, you called me up again tonight

But ooh, this time I'm telling you, I'm telling you

We are never, ever, ever getting back together

We are never, ever, ever getting back together

You go talk to your friends, talk to my friends, talk to me (talk to me)

But we are never ever ever ever getting back together

Ooh, yeah, ooh yeah, ooh yeah

Oh oh oh

I used to think that we were forever ever

And I used to say, "Never say never..."

Uggg... so he calls me up and he's like, "I still love you,"

And I'm like... "I just... I mean this is exhausting, you know, like,

We are never getting back together. Like, ever"

No!

We are never ever ever getting back together

We are never ever ever getting back together

You go talk to your friends, talk to my friends, talk to me

But we are never ever ever ever getting back together

We, ooh, getting back together, ohhh,

We, ooh, getting back together

You go talk to your friends, talk to my friends, talk to me (talk to me)

But we are never ever ever ever getting back together" she finished singing, seeming to have used every corner of the stage and somehow managed to make eye contact with everyone in the restaurant. Her stage presence was incredible, everyone in this place felt a connection and all she did was sing one song. She really was amazing! The crowd erupted into applause once again but this time it was for someone who deserved it a lot more. I clapped as hard as I could, feeling the supportive grin that I couldn't wipe from my face. Seeing her perform like that, it inspired me. I wanna be able to perform and work the stage like she does. I know it will take a while to get there but I knew that little by little with hers and others guidance, I would get there. She walked off the stage and after handing the microphone back, she headed towards the table with everyone staring at her she took a seat just as the food had come out. We started to eat knowing that a few people were still watching us, trying to make ourselves as normal and mundane as any other person here. Hoping that they would get bored and look away, but it never happened.

"So Bella where are you going after your finished here?" she asked curiously.

"Car shopping, I have saved up some money and was gifted a bit so I am getting rid of my beloved truck and getting some type of new car" I explained, trying not to bore her with too many details. I felt slightly sad thinking about the fact that my truck wouldn't be my main form of transport anymore, but it was definitely time. Even coming here today was a struggle and I have to admit being restricted speed wise had slowed down the journey ridiculously. I didn't want anything overly flashy like Rosa-... just something slick and convenient to get around in.

"Do you mind if I join you, I could help you chose and keep you guys company" she offered in an nonchalant way. I was surprised she didn't have any plans after this. I would have thought she would be whisked away at any minute to go and cover her pop star duties. But she was so down to Earth and just seemed like another genuine teenager that just wanted to spend time with someone her age.

"We could definitely use the help, plus company is always great. Which car dealership should we try first?" I asked. She looked thoughtful for a second, as she whispered back to a security guard standing just behind her.

" I say first we go to Audi, Mercedes, then maybe Lotus" she said "and if they don't have anything you like then we'll contemplate where to next?" she asked, repeating the advice she was given by her guard.

"Ok, sounds good. Hopefully I find something without having to go to too many" I say sheepishly, not wanting to drag the girls through multiple car dealerships if I didn't have to.

Taylor raised her hand signaling a waiter over. I slid her a 50 which she grabbed to hand to the waiter she also put a 50 in.

"Keep the change" she said as she smiled at the shocked waiter. We all got up and walked out of the restaurant.

"Well that was fun. Did you have fun Ange?" I asked my best friend who was smiling brightly.

"Yes!" she yelled. I laughed at her enthusiasm. We put our heads down as soon as the flashes started. we all had our arms linked as the security guards surrounded us once again. It took a while to get to the parking lot but we made it.

"Go to Audi first" Taylor said before we unlinked arms and went our separate ways. Most of the media followed Taylor but a few stayed to try to get a response out of me.

"Who are you?" a reporter asked. I ignored him as Taylor had said to do.

"How do you know Taylor?" another asked which I once again ignored. as we reached the truck the media gave up and went to see if Taylor would tell them. I sighed relieved that they had gone. I jumped I the truck as Angela was already inside. The engine roared to life. I pulled out and started in the direction of the closest Audi dealer ship.

....

Tell what you thought of this chapter.

Please vote and comment.

Chapter 6 Car

Hey guys! Here's chapter 5 hope you like! Sorry it took so long just started year nine and have loads of homework already! :(I'll try to update as much as I can though!

Disclaimer: I don't own twilight or any songs featured in this book.

Chapter 6- Car

We made it to Audi and saw Taylor's car a few cars in front of us. I got out of the rusty old truck and walked over trying to make my way through the crowd to Taylor.

Once I got to her she linked arms with me as I was already linking arms with Angela. We made our way to the reception area with the help of Taylor's security guards.

We made our way through the front door and made sure the security blocked paparazzi and fans getting through we made our way over to a smiling car sales man. Once he saw Taylor's face his jaw dropped. He kept opening and closing his mouth like a goldfish trying to decide what to say.

"W-welcome t-to the a-audi dealership. H-how may I h-help you?" he stuttered. I giggled under my breath knowing how it feels to be in his position. I looked over to Angela and she nodded in encouragement. I stepped forward.

"Hi, I've come to buy my self a car. it can be between the price of $100,000 and $500,000. Could you tell me which are best and point out good qualities in the cars as I have never really had much interest in cars and don't know much about them?" I giggled. The salesman looked surprised at the amount I had mentioned but quickly put on a business like face on while nodding his approval. I turned and followed him out the door into the car yard to browse over the flashy looking cars in view. I looked over my shoulder to see Taylor and Angela following me whilst in a deep conversation about their taste in music. I saw Taylor nod in approval at one of Angela's suggestions. I looked to the enter acne of the car yard where Taylor's body guards stood in a line blocking the entry making sure no reporters or fans got through.

"This is the Audi r8 it is a very well known car that everyone dreams to own. It has high quality steering, fantastic handling, fast acceleration, and a very luxurious interior. If you would like we could set you up for a test drive?" he asked. I looked at the car in total awe of it's beauty. It was red with dark grey wheels, leather seats, up to date technology and so much more. It was like a dream. I couldn't believe I could actually afford something as marvelous as this piece of beauty. I nodded in approval and turned to look at my shopping buddies.

"Do you wanna take this masterpiece for a test drive and sign the paperwork after?" I asked them. Angela started nodding enthusiastically, whilst Taylor smiled in silent approval.

"If it is okay we would like to take it for a test drive please?" I asked the salesman politely. he nodded still slightly dazed at seeing Taylor.

"Sure, just need your driver license and I.D. Once you sign a form you can take it for a run" he stated. We followed him into his office to do the necessary requirements to take the piece of art for a test drive.

Ten minutes later I was behind the wheel of this powerful beauty. I enjoyed the way the leather caressed my skin where I was trailing my hand across it. It was so soft, I sunk into the seat a little more getting comfortable. Taylor was in the passenger side with Angela in the small but spacious back seat. I turned the key to hear the engines light purr resound beneath me. I sighed in content, I was grateful it didn't roar to life as my truck had. I stroked the steering wheel lovingly once before reversing out of the car yard and down the streets of Seattle.The car was absolutely amazing! Everything I could of dreamed of I knew instantly it was 'the one'. As we made our way back to the car yard we talked about the pros and cons of the car.

"I am getting it!" I yelled enthusiastically, whilst bouncing up and down on the leather seat in a very Alice like manner. I flinched at the name and instantly put the sad and painful memories back in the box I had collected them all in to keep myself from thinking about them. I instantly scolded myself that I was stronger. I put a smile back on my face deflecting the pain from showing.

"I agree! it's a keeper!" Taylor said. Angela nodded her agreement.

"You have to pick me up for school so I can arrive with you to see how everyone reacts!" Angela giggled.

"Nobody better touch my baby if they like their fingers intact" I said seriously. They laughed and I joined in after a while. I never thought I'd say that about a car.

I pulled into to the car yard and jumped out of the car, luckily my balance was intact. I decided to test my balance a little. I started skipping to the reception door, happy that after signing a few prices of paper and giving out credit details this masterpiece was all mine. I heard Taylor and Angela giggling at me, whist they walked calmly to the door. As soon as we entered we approached the salesman at the front desk. I smiled at him.

"I would like to buy it please?" I asked politely. Grinning in anticipation.

"Sure, come this way so you can sign a few forms and get the payments sorted" he requested whilst gesturing to an empty office. I nodded and gestured for the girls to come too. we walked into the small office. It had white walls and a wooden desk with two chairs placed in front and an office chair behind the desk. There was filing cabinets filling most of the back wall. There was also a couch placed on the right side of the office that Taylor and Angela were getting comfortable on. I saw them start chatting about school and music. I walked up to one of the seats in front of the desk and sat getting comfortable as I knew there was quite a lot of paper work to be completed.

"Would you like anything to eat or drink?" he asked, whilst he pulled out the necessary forms that needed to be filled out. I looked at Taylor and Angela who both shook their heads. I turned back to the salesman who I learnt his name was mark.

"No, but thanks for offering" I stated gratefully. He smiled before getting back to the task at hand. After he explained how to fill in each form and what to put where and getting all the proof of I.D. that was needed he left to tend to another customer while I filled out the rest of the forms.

"Finally, I'm done!" I said in exasperation. as I placed the pen down with a sigh of relief. I was so excited that beautiful red car waiting outside was officially mine. I did a little happy dance which resulted in me nearly falling, we all started laughing at my stupidity. Mark walked in then coming to check how far I had done he seemed a little surprised at how fast I had completed all the forms. He looked through them making sure that everything was answered or written in the right places. After double checking my details and confirming that it had successfully paid, he gave me the keys and the manual. He explained a few important features to look out for and how to work a few technical devices.

I walked outside jumping up and down excitedly. I hopped into my new car rejoicing in the fact it is officially mine. I drove it out front and parked in the available spot behind my truck. I jumped out locked the doors and walked over to Taylor and Angela.

....Please vote and comment the more you vote or comment the faster I update! I need more votes please!Tell me any suggestions you have for this story and I'll take them in consideration and most likely use them in the story.

Bye! :)

Chapter 7 Surprises

Hey guys here's chapter 7! I am sorry I haven't updated I've been busy with test and assignments! I hope you like!

Disclaimer: I do not own twilght or any of the songs featured in this story although I wish I did. :(

Chapter 7- Surprises

"Ange, do you mind taking my car back?" I asked her.

"Sure, I don't mind!" she said enthusiastically. I handed her the keys and she looked down to see the new keys. She looked back up at me in surprise.

"I thought you meant the truck?" she asked surprised. I raised an eyebrow.

"No, but if you really want you can take the truck?" I stated. She immediately started to shake her head. I smiled at the gesture. She started bouncing up and down on the spot in excitement. I looked over to Taylor.

"Soo... I guess this is goodbye at least till a few weeks time" I said sadly to her.

"We need to exchange numbers first!" she exclaimed. She pulled out a piece of paper and asked the security guards, which were currently surrounding us, if any of them had a pen. A dark haired man that was very bulky had pulled out a pen and handed it to Taylor.

"Thank you, Bryan!" Taylor exclaimed. Bryan nodded his head in reply. Taylor ripped the paper into three pieces handing one to us to put both of our numbers on. Whilst, she scribbled down her number on the other two. Angela and I waited patiently to use the pen so we could write ours down. when she finished she handed both of us one piece of paper which had her number written neatly on them. She also gave me the pen. I quickly wrote down my mobile number and home number on the paper I had in my hands. When I was done I handed the pen and paper to Angela. I hugged Taylor goodbye as Angela was writing.

"I may be able to come visit before the talent show sometime to watch you practice and have a little fun! If I have time I will call you before I come!" she exclaimed in excitement. Angela handed the paper to Taylor.

"There yo-" Angela started to say before Taylor pulled her into a hug. she was a bit surprised but hugged her back after a while.

"I'll miss you guys, even though we've only know each other for a few hours! It feels like we've known each other for years!" she exclaimed in a sad tone.

"We'll miss you too,Tay" I said her nickname for the first time. She gave us one last hug before slowly walking off.

"Make sure you call me!" she yelled before she got into her car. We turned around to get to the car we were going to drive.

"Are you sure that you want me to drive your baby?" Angela said a little shyly.

"I'm sure! drive to Charlie's house and I'll drop off the truck them come and join you in the r8. We'll then go to your house after you grab your stuff from the house," I explained the plan I had made. She nodded in understanding. I walked over to the truck, I looked at it and couldn't believe I had loved it. Sure it had charm, but nothing compared to my baby.

'I can't believe she let me drive this work of art. Bella is so nice and un-selfish' I looked around and saw Angela in my car waiting for me. Who said that? I swear I heard someone speak, but there was no one. I shook my head, maybe it was just me.

'What's wrong with bella? she looks confused and scared. maybe I should see if she's ok' I recognised it was angela, but she was inside a car.

'I wonder why those girls haven't left yet' a male voice spoke.

'Should I get it in green or red' a feminine voice said.

'Which direction did Taylor go?' a deep male voice resounded. why can I hear all these voices. No one was near me. What's going on? It's as if I can hear their thoughts, but that would be impossible.

"Are you ok Bella?" Angela yelled from my new car. she was standing outside next to the drivers door. I nodded and tried blocking all the voices in my head. I couldn't tell anyone about this. I need to work out why I am like this. I got in the truck and started driving to Charlie's house thinking about what was happening. To me all the way there.

****************************So that's chapter seven! I hope I can update more over the holidays for you! thank you for voting and commenting! love you!

Vote&CommentXOXO Meg

Chapter 8 Unexpected

Hey guys here's chapter 8! hope you love it!

Disclaimer: I do not own twilight or any of the songs in this fanfic. :(

Chapter 8- Unexpected

How is this possible? What's happening to me? Why can I hear others thoughts? What makes me so special? I'm human aren't I?

All these questions were running through my head. As soon as I drop Angela off I was going to the one place that would let me think all by myself without interruption. The place he used to go to relax by himself. I remembered how to get there and what direction. I'm just hoping I don't get lost.

I kept driving down the high way towards forks. Pushing my truck to go faster. Angela was following me to Charlie's.

'OH MY GOD.... IS THAT AN AUDI R8. My dream car....' I looked up to see a black Mercedes in my rearview mirror. The driver was staring at my new car in a dream like state. I shook my head confused. Why me? I looked back at the road.

I looked into the miles of greenery on the side of the road. I saw a flash of red moving through the trees. I looked closer making sure I don't drive off the road while I'm not watching. It was a blur moving in the forest beside the car.

It looked like THEM when they run. wait! I looked back at the road immediately with wide terrified eyes. The only thing that I know that can move that fast, fast enough to run along side a car would be......

Vampires.

I am being followed by a vampire with red hair! Victoria!

I look back at the forest but don't see any blurs of red. I sigh in relief. Wait! If she's not following me then where is she? I knew she wanted me dead, after all I was the reason her precious James died. What if she stalks me every where until she finds a time to kill me? What if she kills Charlie or Renèe or Angela?

I looked one more time still seeing nothing. I won't let her kill anyone! She has to go past me before she gets to my friends and family! I stepped on the accelerator pushing the truck to go faster. I was now going 110 km/h and knew I was going over the speed limit so I slowed down and settled on a 100 km/h.

I kept glancing out the window the whole drive home. I was also checking that Angela, who was still behind me, was okay and not harmed. I couldn't let victoria kill them.I turned down Charlie's street. I couldn't wait to get to the meadow and try and relax and figure out what's happening to me. there was one thing I knew I couldn't do, I knew I couldn't tell anyone.

I was scared, angry, confused and sad all at the same time. I was more confused when I got home. why was Charlie home so early? I pulled in to the drive way, I saw Angela pull in behind me.

The front door was open, Charlie never leaves the door open. I ran in, what if Victoria got to him already? I ran past the kitchen and into the living room.

Charlie was asleep on the couch. I sighed in relief but that relief was short lived when I heard her chilling voice.

"Well... If it isn't little insignificant Bella and who's this with you?" she asked in overly sweet voice.

"Victoria leave now! I won't let you hurt the people I love! Edward left he doesn't love me! I bet he wouldn't even care if I died! so leave and take your vengeance out on the bastard that killed James NOT me!" I said in a scary and dangerous voice. I knew she wanted to kill me. her mind was full of ways to get revenge and make Edward suffer, 'a mate for a mate' was her final plan. only I knew that I wasn't his mate, he wouldn't of left me if he was.

'She's lying, Edward wouldn't of left her unprotected. He killed one of his own kind to save this waste of space of a human being. He wouldn't just leave her' she thought.

"But he did, he left me, I meant nothing to him. Every day since he left his last words have echoed through my head. 'It will be as if I never existed'. I was nothing but a distraction to his enteral life and I hate him for that. I hate him and hope he keeps his promise to never return!" I yelled in complete rage of what assward has done to me.

"How did you..." she asked, eyes wide with shock.

"I found out I could read minds today. I can feel power surge through me and I'm not sure I'm even human anymore. I don't know what I am, but I'll figure that out after I kill you." I exclaimed my voice laced with menace. she laughed, and looked at me in disbelief.

I looked back at Angela who had wide terrified and confused eyes. she looked into my eyes, I knew I would have to explain when this was over if I survived that is. I could feel power running through my veins, I felt strong, strong enough to kill her.Charlie had stayed asleep through the whole encounter.

Victoria made her way to me, her eyes black and deadly. I glared back feeling absolute rage. she froze, her eyes still locked with mine.

'What?! How?! Her eyes were brown... How did they turn to red?! What is she?!' her mind scream at me. red?! what does she mean?! They couldn't be?! what's happening to me?!

I looked up to see Victoria shake her head and continue to make her way across the room towards me. She looked at Charlie.

'Maybe I should have a little fun first. a three course meal' her mind said in excitement.

"NO!!" I yelled. Suddenly I was in front of a now wide awake charlie. I acted on instinct as I threw my hands up defensively around Charlie.

"Bella, what's going on?" Charlie asked looking around. I couldn't explain right now.

"Later Charlie, for now stay behind me and be quiet!" I said sternly, I could tell he was surprised by the way my voice sounded and immediately shut up. Why did he not question me further. why does my voice sound like that?

"Crash!" The window of the lounge room broke. How did that happen? I glanced over but immediately looked back at Victoria. Angela ran over to stand behind me terrified for her life. I was shaking in rage as Victoria continued to stalk towards me. The room started to shake, but I was to enraged to care. photo frames circled around the room. In the back of my mind I was questioning what was happening and how I was doing it. I felt strength go through my veins. I was thinking of all the ways to kill Victoria. She collapsed as I glared at her. How am I doing this?

"YOU THOUGHT YOU COULD BEAT ME! YOU THOUGHT I WOULD LET YOU KILL MY DAD AND BEST FRIEND! OVER MY DEAD BODY!" My voice deadly and lethal. Victoria was terrified. She backed away slowly. I wasn't going to let her live, not after she threatens the people closest to me. I sent her another wave of pain. She fell to the floor screaming.

Her screams cut off as her body became lifeless and with a flick my wrist she was on fire and everything fell to the ground around us.

I turned to look at Charlie and Angela. They both flinched when I looked at them. I saw my reflection in the hallway mirrors. I gasped at the red eyes with black streaks. I touched just below my eyes to make sure it was my reflection.

"How are your eyes red? How did the room shake and everything float around the room? who was she or what was she? how did you kill her?" Charlie asked. I glanced at the mirror one more time and saw my eyes turning back to brown. I walked towards Charlie and Angela. Looks like it's time for an explanation, even though I don't know some of it myself.I'll start at the beginning... when I met THEM....

....There's chapter 8! hope you like it! so what do you think is wrong with bella? comment on what you think! the more you vote and comment the faster I update! Love you my fans!

Vote,CommentAnd FollowXOXO meg

Chapter 9 Explanation

Hey guys here's chapter 9! Sorry I haven't updated I've had exams,test and essays plus so much more! I've written a fairly long chapter to hopefully make up for that time! Hope you like! Please vote,comment and possibly fan! Love you my readers!

Disclaimer: I do not own twilight or any of the songs featured in this story, unfortunately.

Chapter 9- Explanation

I turned around towards the fire that had spread and was now burning the floorboards. If I can create it, I can destroy it. I opened my palm and tilted it towards the fire trying to see how I could dull the bright flames. Remarkably, the flames started to extract and disappear. Once the flames were gone I looked around at the damaged room.

How am I going to fix this? How did I even do this? There was photo frames laying everywhere around the room. The coffee table was snapped in half. The lounge room window was broken and the floor boards were burnt.

I knew that I had to act on instinct, my gut feeling. So I raised both hands till they were in-line with my shoulders. I faced my palms to the sky and visualized what the room looked like before. I don't know how I did it but I heard things being picked up off the floor. I heard cracks from the floorboards that were fixing themselves and I heard the sound of glass smashing together. I also heard wood binding together, I assumed that was the coffee table.

'What the.....' Charlie thought.

'Wow!' Angela yelled in her mind.

I opened my eyes to see the living room back to the way it used to be. I looked towards Charlie and Angela. They were in even more shock than they were before. I took in a shaky breathe before sitting on the recliner across from them.

"It all started when I met the..." I flinched. Come on Bella you can do this. "Cullens.... they were not like any other human. They were..." I gulped. "different to say the least," I explained. I was stuck, I didn't know if I should tell them or not. What if they don't believe me? Of course they'll believe you after what happened today.

'How are the Cullens different. Is she saying that their not human. That's impossible! But after seeing what bells did today, I don't know what to believe is real or not. For all I know some of my work mates could be superheroes' Charlie thought. I giggled nervously at the thought.

"Bells... What do you mean by 'different'?" Charlie asked. Angela nodded wanting to know what I meant as well. I took another shaky breathe.

"That isn't my secret to tell, it's theirs" I stood up after that statement. " Come on Ange I'll take you home and we'll talk on the way to your house." I said to her. She looked at her watch.

'Shoot... it's 6 already. What does Bella want to talk about' she thought.

"I'll be back to talk to you in roughly 40 minutes. Bye dad" I said to Charlie. I walked out the door after retrieving the keys from Angela. I jumped in the new car and waited for Angela to grab her bags and jumped in my new car.

"What did you want to talk about izzy?" she asked. Izzy? I like it!

"Izzy? I love it! thanks ange!" I said she blushed and looked down. She looked back up at me expectantly.

"Ok, um... I'm not normal obviously and most likely not human," I started to explain while focusing on the road.

"I wish I could tell you what I was. But the problem is, I haven't figured that out myself yet. I'm telling you this because I know I can trust you. Promise you won't tell anyone what you've seen or heard?" I asked her nervously hoping she agrees to keep it confidential. I glanced at her with hope in my eyes. I knew if she told anyone I'd be doomed and have to hide forever.

"I promise I won't tell anyone not even my mum. Please keep me informed, I'll help you find out what you are." she said with hope. I could feel her gaze on my cheek. I was debating if I should drag her any further into what HE called the 'supernatural world'. I considered seeing if I could erase her memory of today's events with my new found powers. But I quickly dismissed the thought. After all I need some one to talk to about these problems, some one trust worthy like Ange.

"Sure, you can help me. But if it get's to dangerous I will have to do something." I warned her.

"What do you mean by 'do something'?" she asked suspiciously. I could feel her curious gaze on my face. I glanced at her and saw she was analysing my facial expressions, which had changed to caution and worry. I quickly replaced my expression to a small smile to not look suspicious.

"Um.... don't worry about it..." I said focusing extra hard on the road. Which was pointless as I had stopped at a red light. I looked at the pedestrians crossing the road. They were staring at my car, Talking and pointing with admiration in their eyes and expressions. I looked at Angela she was raising her eyebrows with her arms crossed. I sighed.

"Erase your memory" I muttered.

"What?" she asked leaning in to hear better. I glanced at the red light before turning back to look at her.

"Erase your memory" I repeated louder this time. I step on the accelerator when I saw the light turn green, refusing to look at her face.

"You would do what? How do you know you could do that?" she asked in surprise.

"I would if it came to your safety. I don't know what I can do yet but I will try. I will experiment tomorrow and Monday afternoon possibly Monday morning too." I said. I parked in front of her house. I could see her family having dinner through the window.

"I want to help!" she pleaded.

"Ange you know what I said about safety. I could accidentally kill you whilst using unknown powers. I can't risk your life, you have people to live for. " I said to her in a serious tone. When I saw the pleading look on her face I sighed in annoyance. Why does she have to make this any harder?

"At school I will tell you everything that happened. I promise... I may even demonstrate some to you after school that's if I find anymore" I said in a tone that ends the subject.

"Okay, that's the best I'm going to get. So see you on Monday Izzy" she replied using my nickname. She grabbed her bags and started to exit my new car.

"Bye Ange. Be safe, if you need anything I'm a phone call away." I said all seriousness left my face only to be replaced by a wide smile.

"Bye Iz"She said shutting the door and walking to her front door. I started driving home knowing I'd have to explain today's events to Charlie next.

Here we go again.....

....

Hey guys hope you enjoy this chappie it's nice to know your opinions on the book so vote and comment please! If you have any ideas or suggestions message me and I'll consider putting them in my book! Love you my readers!

XOXO Meg

Chapter 10 Charlie

Hey guys here's chapter 10! hope you like! Love you my readers!

Disclaimer: I do not own twilight or any of the songs featured in this story.

Chapter 10- Charlie

I got home and parked on my side of the drive way before getting out and locking my baby. I walked towards the house and opened the front door with the hidden key. I walked through and down the hallway. I poked my head through the doorway of the living room. I saw Charlie sitting watching baseball league. He looked to be deep in thought. Thoughts? I haven't heard many in my head lately. Where'd they go?

'What is she? How did she become like this? I will find out and support her if needed. I won't love her any less. I love her just the way she is!' I heard the gruff voice of my father in my head again. I sighed, still doomed with the gift to invade others privacy. Just like Edw-HIM, I flinched thinking about HIM. I shook my head, shaking away the memories.

"Dad, I'm going to get dressed in something more comfortable. I'll talk when I come back okay?" I said. He looked up at me a little surprised. He probably didn't hear me enter.

"Sure Bells, take your time" he said. 'I wonder what she is? An angel maybe?' he thought. I laughed at his 'theory'. I flinched again as the word brought back so many memories. I turned away towards the stairs. I ran up, nearly tripping on the last step. Looks like I still need to work on balance.

I entered my room to collect my toiletries and new winter pajamas. I made my way to the only bathroom.After the shower I brushed my teeth and unknotted my long chestnut brown hair. I braided my hair to the side like Ali- SHE taught me to do. I looked down at the midnight blue pajama set I was wearing. It looked good, especially with my pale skin.I unlocked the bathroom door and after returning my toiletries to my room and putting away my dirty clothes, I made my way back down. I walked into the kitchen and grabbed a bottle of water. I made my way towards the living room, preparing my tired mind for the explanation that would follow. I entered the living room and sat on the recliner that faces Charlie. He immediately turned off the TV knowing this talk was important.

"Dad, I know you have a lot of questions so I'll answer as many as I can because some answers I may not know. Okay, ask one at a time please" I told him.

"What are you?" he asked. I was expecting this question.

"I'm can't tell you because I'm not sure myself" I said as I lowered my head in disappointment. I heard him sigh and felt him rub my shoulder in comfort.

"I'll help you find out but for now do you have any 'theories'?" he asked. I flinched at 'the word' again. I looked back up into his brown eyes.

"I'm not positive but I have three main ideas of what I am" I explained. I looked out the window whilst saying this refusing to meet his eyes.

'What does she believe she is?' Charlie's gruff voice echoed through my head, just when I thought I had peace up there.

"Go on," he said getting a little impatient. I looked at him thinking if I should tell him or not.

"Witch, A Hybrid of some type or a Wizard" I said "but those are just unsure guesses".

I looked at him again and he looked deep in thought.

"I don't think your a wizard and your powers seem to be too strong for a hybrid so the only option that makes sense would be, your a witch" he said. surprisingly he made a lot of sense. I will have to tell Angela our main theory, flinch, tomorrow. I nodded approving of his thought process.

"By the way what are the Cullens if they're not human?" Charlie asked curiously. I sighed thinking we had dropped this subject long ago.

"I can't tell you dad, for your own safety. I'm sorry, I would if I could" I said to him looking down.

"How did you find out?" he asked suspiciously.

"Observing" I said. I wanted to get off this topic as I was starting to feel uncomfortable. I didn't like talking about people behind their backs, even if it was THEIRS. I looked at Charlie and saw his eyes were beginning to droop.

"Do you want dinner before you go to bed?" I asked my tired father. He shook his head whilst yawning.

"I ate something when you were gone" he replied. I nodded and offered a hand to help him off the couch. He took it and I effortlessly pulled him up with my new found strength. He grunted before dragged his feet up the stairs to his bedroom to get some rest.

I looked at the clock on the living room wall. It was only 7:01pm and I was not tired. I made my way to the kitchen and made myself a sandwich. I ate my sandwich and made my way to the stair case deciding to test my abilities further.

I've always wanted to fly..

That's it till next chapter my fellow wattpadders! Vote, comment and possibly fan! If you have any ideas for future characters or plot lines please send me a message and I may use your ideas! Remember the more you vote and comment the more time I make to write! Love you my readers!

XOXO Meg

Chapter 11 Flying Singing and a Surprise Visit

Hey guys here's chapter 11! I hope you like! Love you guys!

Disclaimer: I do not own twilight or any of the songs featured in this book.

Chapter 11- Flying and Singing

I've always wanted to be able to fly. Well here goes nothing. I imagined me hovering above the ground that I'm standing on. I willed myself to move and hover above the first step. I looked down and saw I was hovering over the first step. I was amazed at the new power I have found. I could fly... I lost concentration and felt myself falling towards the steps. I tried to save myself but failed. I put my hands out I front of me and all of a sudden I stopped falling. I was hovering over the steps inches from impact. I sighed in relief that I was saved by my powers. I slowly lowered myself to lay on the steps- which weren't very comfortable.

I decided to be safe for now and walk up the steps. I think that's enough power testing for now. I walked towards my room still in my new pajamas.

A tune started to reside it's self in my head. I couldn't help but sing this song aloud.

"But even if the stars and moon collide,I never want you back into my life.You can take your words and all your lies,Oh oh ohI really don't care"

I really liked these lyrics so I ran the rest of my way to my room. Once I was inside I closed my eyes and imagined the empty song book I left around here some where. I reached out my hand and the book flew into it from it's recently placed spot. I walked towards my desk amased at how powerful I was. I picked up the pen that was left on the small wooden desk and sat down on the old creaky office chair.

I started to write the lyrics I had previously sung. As I wrote these other lyrics started to appear in my head. I continued writing the words out on the empty page. Once I had finished expressing the tune that was in my head I was really tired. I decided that I would read over the lyrics in the morning. I got out of the creaky chair and made my way towards my bed. I tucked my self in and instantly fell asleep.

.... (I was going to end it here but I decided that I would continue going since I haven't updated in a while) ....

I woke up to a loud clutter down stairs. I got up out of my comfortable bed to investigate. I walked down stairs in my pj's and bed hair towards the unknown noise. I went to the area the noise came from knowing that Charlie was out fishing. I peeked around the corner, ready to defend myself if needed.

I saw the back of a feminine figure.

"Mum?!" I yelled in surprise. The figure turned to reveal the face I knew all to well. I screamed and ran towards her and embraced her in my arms. I had longed for the moment to have her in my hold again.

"What are you doing here?" I asked surprised. I pulled away at arms length to look at her. Renae was exactly how I left her. She smiled at me, a smile that I have missed the past few months.

"I thought I'd give you a surprise visit!" She exclaimed in an excited voice. I looked around the kitchen and saw various cooking items placed on the once isolated bench.

"Mum, are you attempting to cook again? You do remember what's happened the past few times don't you?" I asked worried that she might nearly burn the house down or give me food poisoning. She started to laugh as she made her way around the kitchen effortlessly, like she knew where everything was.

"I took cooking classes in my time in Jacksonville" she said smiling, " I really love it there, so many opportunities to chose from."

"That's great Mum, so how's Phil?" I asked curiously wondering why he wasn't here.

"Playing, training and coaching as usual" she said smiling at the subject. I was happy for my mother she found love at last.

"I heard about the break up Bella, how have you been?" she asked in concern whilst cracking an egg on the stove.

'I hope she's okay and hasn't gone into the whole teenage's first love tragedy break down' Her thought echoed in my head. I thought that I got rid of this power at least for now when u don't need it. I respect others privacy not invade it stupid privacy invading power. I snapped out of the useless and crazy talk I had to my power when I realised how insane I sound. Instead I attempted to answer her question.

"I'm fine, really. Just a little shocked that he would lie like he did. I was just a toy in his little collection, a nobody. Some one he could practice his little act on." I expressed my feelings to my mother. She looked at me with sympathy in her eyes which were surrounded by laugh lines. I smiled and turned towards the stairs.

"I'm going to go get dressed and brush the hay stack on top of my head" I said over my shoulder. I heard her laugh and continued to make my way up the stairs to my room. I ran in and grabbed some new skinny jeans ,a red crop top and my new leather jacket. I was going to change my fashion starting from today. I made my way to the only bathroom and locked the door. I turned on the shower and hopped in. I started to sing the tune that I wrote down last night.

"You wanna playYou wanna stay You wanna have it allYou started messing with my headUntil I hit a wallMaybe I should of knownMaybe I should of knownThat you would walkYou would walkOut the doorHey!"

I jumped out of the shower and dried myself. I could still here mum cooking downstairs and I hoped that she doesn't burn the house down with her awful cooking skills. I got dressed and couldn't be bothered to brush my hair but I knew if I didn't it would be impossible to get out later.

Maybe I should see if I can make my hair look decent by using my powers. I closed my eyes and imagined my hair up in a high ponytail. I snapped my fingers like they do on all the witch shows and hoped for the best. I opened my eyes to see my hair fully dry and unknotted. It was up in a perfect high ponytail. I sighed and made my way towards my mother preparing myself for the worst.I walked into the kitchen and saw two plates on the table filled with eggs, bacon and toast. I must say it looked appealing and hopefully safe.

I saw mum drying the frying pan before placing it back in it's original place. She turned and let out a gasp of surprise seeing me at the door way. She instantly relaxed when she saw who it was.

I made my way towards the table and inspected the food closely, I took a sniff at it and decided it was safe.

"Bella I swear it's safe, I didn't give you food poisoning or whatever" she exclaimed whilst laughing,"What are you wearing?"

"Um... my new clothes, I guess?" I asked in question.

"They suit you" she complemented whilst I blushed.

"Thanks" I said in gratitude.

I started to eat and mum came and joined me. Once I was finished I took my plate to the sink.

"Thanks mum that was great!" I exclaimed. I heard the doorbell ring and turned towards the front door.

"I'll get it!" I exclaimed towards mum who was looking at me curiously. I walked towards the door confused to who it was. I opened the door to two female figures.

"Taylor! Ange! What are you doing here?" I exclaimed whilst hugging them I looked over Taylor's shoulder and saw with my enhanced sight, a figure in the distance. They were looking this way with familiar yellow eyes. I gasped and instantly pulled back from the hug and dragged them inside. They looked at me confused and worried, but they quickly shook it off.

"We came to practice since Taylor was free today" Angela exclaimed.

"Have you told her yet?" I asked Angela, referring to Taylor.

"Told me what?" Taylor exclaimed in curiosity. We heard a gasp come from behind us.

"Is that Taylor Swift?" mum exclaimed. I turned to see mum standing in the doorway of the kitchen.

"Yep that's me. I am here to see Bella here. May I ask your name?" Taylor spoke formally. I started to laugh at the strange interaction.

"I'm Renae, Bella's mum, nice to meet you Taylor. Not to be rude but what are you doing here?" Mum asked kindly.

"Nice to meet you Renae, I'm here to practice singing with a very talented Bella" She said whilst smiling at me as I blushed.

"Bella you can sing? Why didn't you tell me?" She exclaimed a little hurt. This whole time Angela was looking at me confused, probably on why mum was here.

"Mum you only arrived this morning, I was not expecting a surprise visit. I have also been really busy sorting things out and it slipped my mind to tell you. I'm sorry!" I said in apology. Taylor looked at me confused.

"My parents are split up. I lived with mum until about a year and a half ago, when I moved in with my dad. So mum has travelled all the way from Jacksonville, Florida to see me." I explained to Taylor. She nodded in understanding.

"Mum can you take the guest to the living room and offer snacks whilst I grab something from up stairs?" I asked in hope. She nodded and escorted Taylor and Angela to the lounge room. I ran upstairs to fetch my new song book to show Taylor and hopefully attempt to write another.

I opened the door and instantly knew I wasn't alone. Lying on my bed was a sobbing Alice Cullen.

"Alice?!" I exclaimed.

She looked up at me with dead and emotionless eyes.

"What happened to you?"........

....There is chapter 11! Sorry I took so long to update! Please vote, comment and possibly follow! Love you guys!

XOXO Meg

Chapter 12 Alice

Hey guys here's chapter 12! Hope you like it! Vote and comment if you do! The songs Bella writes that she claims are her own are in real life actual songs sung by various artist!

Disclaimer: I do not own twilight or any of the songs featured in this story.

Chapter 12- Alice

"Help.... me....." Alice whispered in a weak and sorrow filled voice. I rushed towards her and saw her now black eyes staring at me.

"You need to hunt! Go now before you starve and once your done if you need me come in here and I'll let you stay if needed." I told her urgently, concerned about her. I know she left me but I knew if she needed help I couldn't deny it after all the helpful things she did for me.

(Important AN- if you are wondering why she doesn't read thoughts as often it is because that power only comes out when she is concentrating on her powers).

I sighed relieved when I saw she had disappeared to go and hunt. I grabbed the notebook and ran down the stairs. I got to the lounge room and saw Taylor, Angela and Mum talking and laughing. I took a deep breath to calm myself before making my way into the room and sitting down next to Taylor on the three men couch. They all looked towards me in expectation. I handed Taylor the book and she opened it to the first page and started reading.

"This is really good! What inspired this song?" she asked curiously.

"My first break up." I explained. She nodded.

"Tough times," she said understanding what I was going through. She hugged me reassuringly in a sisterly way.

"Bella could you sing for me?" Renae asked me, looking with pleading eyes.

"Um..... What song?" I asked a little nervous.

"Torn by Natalie Imbruglia" she suggested. I knew this song as mum would play it around the house regularly. I took a deep breath and prepared myself to sing yet another song.

"I thought, I saw a man brought to lifeHe was warm, he came around and he was dignifiedHe showed me what it was to cryWell, you couldn't be that man I adoredYou don't seem to knowSeem to care what your heart is forBut I don't know him anymore

There's nothing where he used to lieThe conversation has run dryThat's what's going onNothing's fine, I'm tornI'm all out of faithThis is how I feelI'm cold and I am shamedLying naked on the floorIllusion never changedInto something realI'm wide awake and I can seeThe perfect sky is tornYou're a little late, I'm already torn

So I guess the fortune teller's rightShould have seen just what was thereAnd not some holy lightIt crawled beneath my veinsAnd now I don't care, I had no luckI don't miss it all that muchThere's just so many thingsThat I can touch, I'm torn

I'm all out of faithThis is how I feelI'm cold and I am shamedLying naked on the floorIllusion never changedInto something realI'm wide awake and I can seeThe perfect sky is tornYou're a little late, I'm already torn, torn

There's nothing where he used to lieMy inspiration has run dryThat's what's going onNothing's right, I'm torn

I'm all out of faithThis is how I feelI'm cold and I am shamedLying naked on this floorIllusion never changedInto something realI'm wide awake and I can seeThe perfect sky is torn

I'm all out of faithThis is how I feelI'm cold and I'm ashamedBound and broken on the floorYou're a little late, I'm already torn, torn"

I sang the last note to a perfect pitch. I had missed singing this song and can relate to it much more now.

I looked up and saw my mum smiling proudly at me. I laughed at the goofy smile that had taken place on Taylor's face. Angela was in awe yet again. I stood up when I felt a presence in my room.

"I need to go to the bathroom be back in a second" I lied to them. I made my way to the stair case and made sure no one could see me before clicking my fingers and appearing at the top. I am really improving at using my powers. I walked towards my bedroom door and opened it slowly to reveal Alice rocking in the rocking chair that was situated in the corner of my room. She was curled up in a ball with torn and bloodied clothes stuck to her skin. She looked at me with pleading eyes begging for my help. I walked towards her slowly soaking in that she was really here. I reached out my arms and she immediately ran into my embrace.

"I'm here, I'll protect you. I'll help you as much as I can ok?" I said whilst stroking her short spiky hair.

"Ally before I can help I have to know what happened?" I asked worriedly.

"Jas..... per.... le-left... me..." she stuttered out in a depressed and sorrow filled voice.

"It's okay, I'll help you through this. First you need a new set of clothes. Come on Ally, I even have a all new closet from the money you left me." I said hoping to make her feel a little better. I grabbed her ice cold hand and dragged her towards the closet.

"Pick whatever you like. I have to go downstairs but I swear I'll be back ok Ally?" I said in a gentle voice. She nodded her head and started to look through my closet weakly. I kissed her cheek and hugged her in a sisterly way before making my way back down. I walked back into the lounge room.

"Um...... So what song shall we start to practice?" I asked Taylor. She shook her head.

"I decided that maybe instead you could show me around then we could get to know each other more. Is that okay?" She asked me.

"Okay, Um.... well come with me and I'll show you around the house" I said.

"Alice... hide I have guest who want to look around the house" I whispered so the others couldn't hear but I knew she could.

"Okay well this is obviously the lounge room and through this door is the kitchen" I explained whilst walking through the familiar house with Taylor, Angela and Renae following me. We all walked up the stair case and walked to the end of the hallway.

I opened Charlie's bedroom door.

"This is Charlie, My dad's room" I explained. I shut the door and opened the bathroom door.

"This is the ONLY bathroom, otherwise known as the public toilet" I said. The girls laughed whilst I was hoping Alice had hidden well. I tried to feel where abouts in my room she was with my powers. I felt some one underneath my bed. I opened the door to my room with confidence knowing she was out of sight.

"This is my lovely bedroom" I said with confidence knowing Alice was under the bed I purposely avoided looking under so the others wouldn't get suspicious.

"Bella why is some one in your room?" Renae whispered to me whilst the other two girls searched my closet. I looked towards her with wide eyes.

"How did you know?" I asked in disbelief.

"Where do you think you got your witch genes from?" She asked me.

"Your the reason I'm a witch?" I asked.

"Yep but your a lot stronger then your meant to be. I wonder why? But do you know the person under your bed?" She asked.

"Yes, I asked her to hide there. She needed help and I owe it to her." I whispered cautious for the other girls not to here me.

"Who is she? What is she? And why is she here?" Renae asked still a little worried. I looked over towards the other girls and saw them looking through my cd's. It would of been a much better day if I did what I originally planned, power training.

"Her name is Alice Cullen, HIS sister and my best friend. I'm swore to protect their secret so I can't answer the second question. She needs help because she's going through a tough time right now and she helped me through a lot of my hard times. So I'm going to help her no matter what" I whispered.

"Just tell her Bella" I heard Alice whisper from under the bed in a tortured voice. I didn't question her request and debated how I was going to tell her.

"Alice and her family including Edward are vampires. Alice is here because Jasper he supposed mate left her." I explained. Renae nodded her head.

"Thank you, and Alice stay as long as you need. If Bella trust you I will too." She said towards my best friend.

"So Bella where shall we get to know each other?" Taylor asked.

"Um..... why don't we go down to the lounge room because I'm expecting another visitor" I suggested they all looked curious of who it was.

"You start making your way down, I'll be there in a second." I said to them. They all nodded and left my mum looked at me before she left. She gave me a look that told me to be careful. As soon as the door was closed Alice appeared on the bed in a tight long sleeved black shirt and high waisted shorts.

"Who else is visiting?" she asked.

"You are. I want you to go to the front door, knock and join our session. Please it will make you feel better." I pleaded. She nodded weakly.

"Please don't be sad sis." I said in a kind voice. She looked at me surprised.

"You st- still think of me as a sister?" She asked in disbelief. I nodded and she hugged me tightly.

"Can't breathe" I said jokingly. She laughed a weak laugh.

"That's what I wanna hear" I said smiling down at her small frame. She gave me a small smile back.

"What's this about witches?" She asked confused.

"Um...... Roughly a day after you left I found out I had powers like fire control and telekinesis." I said. She looked surprised.

"Um..... before I go and you knock on the door. I need to tell you something. I kinda killed Victoria with these powers" I said. Alice looked at me with wide eyes.

"H-how?" she asked confused.

"I guess I'm really strong" I said.

"I have to go before they get suspicious I'll meet you at the door on your knock." I said. I clicked my fingers and my hair was let down in a wavy style. This would give me an alibi. I looked at Alice before I left and she looked impressed with my little stunt. I checked to see if any one was near the bottom of stairs and saw only Angela about to make her way up. I snapped my fingers and appeared at the bottom. Angela jumped in surprise at me appearing next to her.

"Don't do that to me... Where were you I was just about to come and make sure you were okay" She said worry still hidden in her voice.

"I'm fine, just refreshed myself a little" I explained pointing to my hair. I heard the door bell ring and pointed to the door.

"That would be the guest I was expecting" I exclaimed. Angela looked at me curiously wondering who it was. Taylor and Mum made their way out to see who it was, though I assumed mum knew already. I opened the front door and I heard Angela gasp behind me.

"Alice?!" Angela yelled before running and hugging her. Taylor looked on confused. I giggled at Angela before looking at Alice, she looked like she was feeling a little better.

"Come here Ally" I said. She hugged me again.

"Welcome, stay as long as you like okay?" I said to her.

"Thanks Izzy" She said her voice still weak.

"Taylor this is Alice, her brother is my ex" I said wincing at the subject.

"Nice to meet you Alice" Taylor said shaking her hand. Taylor winced a little at how cold it was.

"Why is Taylor Swift in your house?" Alice asked me in a whisper.

"Long story short... I'm a talented singer apparently" I whispered back. She nodded when her eyes glazed over Angela, Taylor and Renae looked at her strangely in her still state.

"Um.... well we'll leave Alice to have her vi- day dream whilst we go to the lounge room. Trust me when I say that when she day dreams it's hard to get her back to earth." I laughed trying to lighten the mood and so no one was suspicious of Alice's actions.

"She will snap out of it in a minute in the mean time let's go to the lounge room and start the interrogation" I joked pulling the attention away from a stationary Alice. I escorted them to the living room all of them still a little suspicious of Alice's actions.

"So Taylor What's your favourite colour?" I asked to distract her from her thoughts.

"Um.... Gold. Angela what's your favourite food?" she asked Angela.

"Oh... um.... Italian?" she said it like a question. I nodded in approval.Why was Alice taking so long she usually doesn't take this long?

"Bella who's your celebrity crush?" Angela asked me.

"Um....uh.... Niall from one direction" I said blushing. Taylor and Angela laughed and Mum raised her eyebrows.

"Does any one want a drink?" I asked wanting to check on Alice.

"Water" they all replied at once.

"Okay, be back soon" I said before rushing from the room.

I came into the kitchen when I didn't see her in the hallway and saw her pacing inside the kitchen.

"Alice what's wrong?" I asked concerned.

"They want me... They're trying to find me... what should I do?" Alice whispered.

Who's trying to get my Ally?

....There's chapter 12! Who do you think wants Alice? What's going to happen next? Vote and comment to find out.Love you my readers!

Vote, Comment &Follow

XOXO Meg

Chapter 13 The Vision

Hey readers here's chapter 13! Hope you like! sorry I took so long the chapter got deleted some how! what's even creepier is it mysteriously deleted itself on Friday the 13th!

Disclaimer: I do not own twilight or any of the songs featured in this story.

Chapter 13- The Vision

"Who?" I ask a scared Alice.

"The.... V-Volturi" she says in a shaky whisper slight disgust in her tone. I nodded remembering what little I know about them.

"Well then let them come, I won't allow them to take you. I will do what ever it takes to help you. Including power training" I said pouring the 4 glasses of water.

"No Bella! This is the Volturi we are talking about! They all hold power that can kill their enemies with little fight! You would be dead with in minutes! I will just leave and give myself up...." she whispered the last part.

"DON'T YOU DARE!!" I yelled I'm a very demanding tone. She looked down contemplating.

"If you do that I will track you down with my powers and drag you back. Even if that means facing the Volturi!" I threatened, honesty clinging to my every word. She nodded in defeat.

"Now let's go and talk to the girls we'll talk about this later" I said whilst kissing her cheek reassuringly. I grabbed the glasses of water and balanced all 4 precariously in my hands. I started walking towards the living room. When I was halfway through the kitchen I felt a glass slipping.

Before I could catch it it started to make it's journey towards the ground. I instantly imagined the glass hovering still full with no spillages. The falling glass immediately stopped inches from the ground. I sighed in relief, and slowly made the cup rise and hover through the air until it reached a shocked Alice. I controlled her hand to grab the hovering glass becoming impatient.

"How did you control the glass and I?" she asked in shock.

"I have my ways or powers" I said winking before walking into the lounge room with Alice following behind.

"There you guys are" Mum said whilst I placed the glasses on the table. I saw Alice do the same. I sat on the love seat and felt Alice join me. I smiled at her reassuringly.

"Cheer up Ally" I whispered whilst giving her a side hug. She smiled as I pulled away. I could tell she was glad to have me here by her side.

"So shall we start the game now? Or do you want a tour around forks?" I asked Taylor. Taylor considered her options.

"Could we get to know each other whilst having a tour around" She replied.

"Tay, always finding a way to get the best of both worlds. Both it is!" I exclaimed with a smile on my face. Now for the tour...

*********************************Sorry it's so short I thought that I would upload a short one! Next chapter will be longer, promise! hope you like! If you have any suggestions for the next chapter or future chapter send me a message or leave a comment! If you want to write the next chapter just tell me over message and I'll give you my email! Up to you readers!

Vote,Comment & FanLove Meg XOXO

Chapter 14 Tour

Hey guys here's chapter 14. If you are wondering why they haven't told Taylor yet is because they are not entirely sure she's trust worthy. Hope you like it!

Disclaimer: I do not own twilight or any of the songs featured in this chapter.

Chapter 14- Tour

I lead everyone outside and we decided to walk around the small town as there were too many to fit in a car. We slowly walked through the small streets of forks occasionally pointing at familiar buildings and landmarks. We chat along the relaxing walk and got to know each other.

I saw an ice cream shop in the distance and my stomach instantly rumbled.

"Guys do you want some ice cream, I've heard this shop serves really good ice cream." I suggested hope filling my voice.

"Sure" they all replied even Alice who had a slight look of disgust on her small petite face. I giggled at her expression and started walking towards the small brick store. The sign said " Lindalicious Ice-Cream". I laughed at the sign and knew the owner must be named Linda.

I walked up the red brick steps and into the small and well organised shop. I looked around and saw various lollies displayed across the wall, brightening the room with their bright colours. I looked towards the long counter and saw lots of different ice-cream flavours displayed through the clear glass.

I scanned all the flavours and was drawn to the flavour of my desire, cookies and cream. I licked my cherry red lips and walked up to the register leaving the others to choose and buy the flavour of their choice. I approached the elderly women standing behind the beige bench and smiled warmly.

"Hello, welcome to Lindalicious ice-cream. How may I help you?" she said in a friendly voice.

"Um... could I get a waffle cone with cookies and cream ice-cream, two scoops." I said as she wrote it down on a notepad in elegant writing. I spotted a coffee machine placed behind her slim body. "And a small hot chocolate please" I added smiling as the women continued to scrawl neatly on the lined page.

"Is that all love?" she asked sweetly. I flinched at the pet name. That's what HE called me.

"Yes, thank you very much" I said in a friendly tone.

"That will be $6.50 please" she said sweetly. I grabbed my new purse and grabbed a ten dollar note out.

"Keep the change" I said. She smiled gratefully at me with slight wrinkles covering her small face. She made her way behind the counter and served my ice-cream and made my hot chocolate whilst the others wondered around the undersized store picking up objects they like. I grabbed my order and sat on the padded seat and started to lick my ice-cream whilst my hot chocolate started to cool off.I saw the others go up to the counter and order their treats and pay. They all joined me at the glass table that held a vase and menu in the centre. We all waited for the orders to be completed and sat around the table getting to know each other and laughing at each others stories and jokes. When the orders arrived we all sat quietly eating the sweets in our hands.

Once we were done we returned our cups although Alice had nothing to return as she didn't order anything, we then thanked the women. I could tell Angela was suspicious of Alice because of what I said earlier. I could literally see the wheels turning in her head and I knew it wasn't long until she took one more step into the supernatural world, I could tell Alice noticed as well.

We walked out of the stall and started to journey back to the house, satisfied with our walk through town. Along the way there was more questions thrown at me and everyone else. Once we reached the house it was getting late and I knew they would have to head home soon. We stopped at a large rock close to the house and sat watching the sunset still chatting amongst ourselves.

Once it started to get cold we made our way inside and Taylor called her driver to pick her up. I volunteered to take Angela back home to her awaiting family. We sat on the couches waiting for Taylor's driver to show up. I saw a black car park smoothly in front of the house and a men wearing all black exit the fancy car.

"That would be me" Taylor said, disappointment colouring her tone.

"Bye Tay" I said a little sad to see her go.

"Bye Bella, keep practicing and I will see you at the talent competition" she said whilst pulling me into a tight hug. She did this to everyone including Alice and Renae. She opened the front door and waved before leaving and jumping into the back seat of the fancy car.

I turned towards Angela and signaled her to follow me out only to get stopped.

"Not so fast, could you please sing another song before you go?" Mum said.

"Okay....um.... what song?" I said a little nervous.

"Who Knew by Pink" she said. This was her favourite song and it was by her favourite singer too. I nodded, I could relate to this song.

"You took my handYou showed me howYou promised me you'd be aroundUh huhThat's rightI took your wordsAnd I believedIn every-thingYou said to meYeah huhThat's right

If someone said three years from nowYou'd be long goneI'd stand up and punch them outCause they're all wrongI know betterCause you said foreverAnd everWho knewRemember when we were such foolsAnd so convinced and just too coolOh noNo no

I wish I could touch you againI wish I could still call you friendI'd give anything

When someone said count your blessings now'fore they're long goneI guess I just didn't know howI was all wrongThey knew betterStill you said foreverAnd everWho knewYeah yeah

I'll keep you locked in my headUntil we meet againUntil weUntil we meet againAnd I won't forget you my friendWhat happened

If someone said three years from nowYou'd be long goneI'd stand up and punch them outCause they're all wrong and

That last kissI'll cherishUntil we meet againAnd time makesIt harderI wish I could rememberBut I keepYour memoryYou visit me in my sleep

My darlingWho knewMy darlingMy darlingWho knewMy darlingI miss youMy darlingWho knewWho knew"

I sang every note to the perfect pitch. I looked around and saw everyone with a tear in their eye except Alice but you could tell she was touched by the emotions I put into the song. I felt a warm liquid run down my cheek as the memories of him flooded my mind. I caught the liquid on my hand that was shaking slightly. I knew it was a waste of time to mourn someone who was never coming back. I immediately rubbed my red eyes to get rid of the tears still sitting their.

"Okay that was a little too deep for my liking. Come on Ange let's go" I said holding back the tear ducts threatening to escape. I'm so pathetic, crying over long lost memories. I grabbed my keys and opened the front door. I got into the car and sunk into the leather seats. I felt a presence join me in the passenger side.

"Are you okay Bella?" Angela's sweet voice asked.

"Yeah, just got caught up in the lyrics" I giggled half heartedly. She sighed not believing me, I turned up the radio and heard the opening notes to Clare De Lune. I fumbled with the radio trying to change the station as the memories yet again flooded my mind. I found the right switch on the complicated radio and turned it to a different station.

The rest of the car ride was silent as no one dared to talk. Although Angela did look curious why I changed the radio station so quickly. I pulled up to the familiar house and parked out front.

"Bye Ange, see you tommorow. Have a nice sleep and don't let the bed bugs bite" I said getting my enthusiasm back. She smiled seeing that I was getting back to myself again.

"See you later Alligator" she said smiling.

"In a while crocodile" I said whilst giggling. She hopped out of the car and walked across the freshly trimmed lawn and up to the doorway. She turned back and waved at me through the tinted windows. I put the window down.

"I'll pick you up tommorow!" I yelled. I saw her nod and walk inside. I could see Katherine at the window waving so I waved back before doing the window back up and driving home again.

*****************************There is chapter 14 for you readers! Hope you like! make sure to suggest your ideas or suggestions in the comments or message me! Continue reading!

Vote, Comment, Fan &Suggest

XOXO Meg

Chapter 15 Talk

Hey guys here's chapter 15! Thank you all soooooo much for reading my book, it means a lot! Hope you like it! Vote, comment, suggest and fan!

Disclaimer: I don't own twilight or any of the songs featured in this chapter.

Chapter 15- Talk

I got home and surprisingly wasn't tired. I got out of the flashy luxurious car and closed the door. I walked up the steps and unlocked the front door. Charlie still wasn't home so I assumed he was staying at billy's and left a message on the home phone because he didn't know my new iPhone's number. I walked into the kitchen and could hear Alice walk in behind me.

"Renae left to her hotel and said she will be back tomorrow after school" She explained the missing presence of my mother. I nodded and started to heat up left overs for my dinner since I had no one else to cook for.

"Are you attending school tomorrow?" I asked her turning around to look in her amber eyes. She hesitated as a thoughtful look appeared over her face she obviously hadn't thought about it.

"I guess? If you want? I mean it looks like I will be staying for a while..." I cheered and hugged her, she hugged me back with her small arms. The microwave interrupted our moment. I pointed my finger at it and the door opened, I concentrated on bringing the container that held leftovers from last nights dinner to hover across to the table and found the task surprisingly easy.

Each day I could feel my powers growing stronger. I had a theory that it all started on my eighteenth birthday and the anger of him leaving made me a stronger witch.. Or the venom left in my bloodstream from James. My eyes lit up at the idea that popped into my mind. Alice gave me a questioning look at my sudden change of expression.

"What is it Bella?" Alice asks curiously.

"I have a theory... you know how I am a strong witch?" she nods signaling to continue, "what if the venom from James had affected my witch genes and made me stronger?"

She thought of the theory in her head for a while and nodded.

"That's actually quite possible" She said. I sat down at the table and ate my dinner with Alice sitting across from me. She looked out the window with a sad look on her small face. I willed myself to enter her mind to see what made her this way.

* Flashback in Alice's Head *

"Alice, I... I've found my true mate and it's not you.... We are what are known as false mates.... Your real mate is out there waiting for you.... I'm sorry.... I'll leave tomorrow.... I'm so sorry, you deserve true love Alice... I hope you find it.... Bye Alice.... I'll miss you...." Jasper said in a sad tone. I watched him walk out the door, out of my life, our life together. I felt lonely, I felt unworthy and self conscious. I felt broken.....

* end *

I pulled out of her mind and wiped the tears that had fallen. I clicked my fingers and got rid of the empty dish in front of me wishing for it to be clean and away. I grabbed Alice's hand and pulled her into a tight hug. I felt her sob into my shoulder, releasing her bottled up feelings. I pulled her upstairs into my room and sat her on the bed. I laid down beside her and pulled her into a comforting side hug and allowed her to cry for hours, just being there for her in her time of need. Every time she looked at me I could tell she was grateful I was there to comfort her.

"I'm going to have a human moment. If you want you can take a shower after me and get cleaned up. Take any clothes you want from my closet. I'll be back in a few minutes Ally" I said once she settled down. She nodded and curled up into a ball on my bed. As I showered all I could think about is how much pain Alice is in and ways I as a friend could help her overcome it. I got dressed in my pajama's and exited the bathroom. I entered my room and noticed Alice was picking out an outfit from my new closet.

"I like your new style" she said in a whisper. I smiled, that was the Alice I knew. She gave me a small smile back and walked gracefully to the door and into the bathroom. I got into the warm comfortable bed and set the alarm for tomorrow, school. I laid there contemplating what would happen tomorrow.

I felt Alice enter the room again and immediately opened my arms, welcoming her to lay with me so I could comfort her. In a blur motion she was laying in my arms on the bed. As soon as she was comfortable I fell asleep, anticipating the oncoming day.

****

Sorry readers! But here's chapter 15! I'm hoping to update more often! Sorry it took so long and I promise the next chapter will be longer! Love you guys!

IMPORTANT: The reader that I think gives the best comment get's a summary of what is coming upon the next chapter via message. Good Luck!

Vote,Comment,Suggest &Follow

XOXO Meg

Chapter 16 School

- -

Here's chapter 16! Another chapter, wow can't believe how far this book has gone! Thank you readers for giving me support to continue! Make sure to suggest any ideas you have for this story!

Disclaimer: I do not own twilight or any of the songs featured in this book. :(

Chapter 16- School

The next day I got up to the annoying sound of my beeping alarm clock. I hit it and got out of the warm duvet. I took a deep breathe and smelt the mouth watering scent of pancakes. I hurried to get dressed in black ripped skinny jeans, a galaxy top and new high top black converse. I applied make up that I learnt how to do from Alice, I also curled my hair in bouncy curls with my new curler. I ran down the stairs and into the kitchen as I felt my stomach growl.

I saw Alice place a plate that held three perfectly cooked pancakes with golden syrup coating them on the table. I licked my pink coated lips and immediately started digging in after thanking Alice. I finished and rubbed my now full stomach.

"They were amazing Ally" I said with gratitude. I put the plate down and clicked my fingers and it was clean. I loved not having to wash up, saves water as well. I turned and realised I forgot my bag and phone so I raised my hands and imagined the items I wanted and immediately felt them pop up into my hands, now I was ready.

"Are you ready?" I asked Alice. She nodded whilst I assessed her clothing choices. She was wearing dark blue tights, a cropped jumper that said 'pineapple dance' and black ankle boots. I started to walk out of the house with my keys in hand with Alice following behind me.

Once I locked the door I jumped in the car and started the engine with Alice sitting quietly in the passenger seat. I started to drive to Angela's house and turned the radio up. I yet again recognised the song playing, Girl on fire by Alecia Keys.

"She's just a girl and she's on fireHotter than a fantasy, lonely like a high-wayShe's living in a world and it's on fireFilled with catastrophe, but she knows she can fly awayOhhhh oh oh oh ohShe got both feet on the groundAnd she's burning it downOhhhh oh oh oh ohShe got her head in the cloudsAnd she's not backing downThis girl is on fire...This girl is on fire...She's walking on fire...This girl is on fire...

Looks like a girl, but she's a flameSo bright, she can burn your eyesBetter look the other wayYou can try but you'll never forget her nameShe's on top of the worldHottest of the hottest girls sayOhhhh oh oh oh

We got our feet on the groundAnd we're burning it downOhhhh oh oh oh ohGot our head in the cloudsAnd we're not coming downThis girl is on fire...This girl is on fire...She's walking on fire...This girl is on fire...

Everybody stares, as she goes by'Cause they can see the flame that's in her eyesWatch her when she's lighting up the nightNobody knows that she's a lonely girlAnd it's a lonely worldBut she gon' let it burn, baby, burn, baby

This girl is on fire...This girl is on fire...She's walking on fire...This girl is on fire...Oh, oh, oh, oh ohhhh oh oh oh ohhh oh oh oh ohhhh... [4x]She's just a girl and she's on fire"

I sang every note to the perfect frequency. I also dedicated the song to Alice who looked like she would be crying if she could. I pulled up to Angela's house whilst giving Alice's hand a tight squeeze.

I saw Angela run down her drive way and open the back door. As soon as she was buckled in I started driving to school.

"Morning Ange, How are you this fine day?" I asked politely.

"Great, and you lovely ladies?" she replied.

"Good" Alice and I replied.

"Bella the talent contest is coming up in two weeks" Angela informed me.

"Yeah, I still need to practice" I replied.

"I also need to do the power training I was supposed to do," I whispered. Alice looked at me curiously so I mouthed 'You'll see' to her. She nodded still looking curious. I saw Alice's eyes glaze over and I knew I had to distract Angela but I also tuned into Alice's thoughts to see the vision.

"Hey Angela what are you writing your English essay on?" I asked to keep her occupied.

Vision

I saw Bella standing in the middle of a field with her hands to the sky. It started to rain after a short while. I felt the cold liquid soak my clot hes."Bella could you try maybe sun or even snow, why rain?" She turned around with blue eyes caused by the change in weather. She nodded at my request and I saw her eyes turn white and saw small white flakes start to fall from the grey clouds up above. With my enhanced vision I could see the individual patterns of the small white wonders.

I felt the wind pick up and the snow swirled around us then suddenly it stopped and the sun started to show.

"Why did you stop? I was enjoying the snow" I whined.

"Cold" She said.

"Why don't you use your witch powers and wish for a jumper" I exclaimed.

"A witch?" I heard a voice come from the forest. In the blink of an eye I was standing protectively in front of Bella.

"What do you want Jane?"

End of Vision

I gasped at the future lied a head of us.

What are we going to do?

*******************************Hey guys! Sorry I haven't been updating I'm getting kinda busy! But hope you like it I am thinking of making a sequel, what do you think?

Vote,Comment,Fan&Suggest

XOXO Meg

Chapter 18 Catch Up With The Past

Hey guys heres's chapter 18! Hope you enjoy!

Disclaimer: I do not own twilight or any of the songs featured in this chapter they belong to their designated owners.

Chapter 18- Catch Up With The Past

"Forget the vision Bella, we'll worry about it later" Alice whispered softly. I nodded my head showing I heard and I agreed. We pulled into the school parking lot and I nodded to Angela and Alice.

I felt the stares of all the students as I exited the flashy car, but one student in particular caught my attention. I gasped in surprise at the unexpected visitor, staring into my brown eyes. I felt Alice stiffen beside me, one question was echoing through my head... Why is she here?

The blonde started to strut her path towards us. I saw someone else I missed dearly appear from the crowd and link arms with her.

"Emmett.... Rosalie" I whispered in greeting. Rosalie raised her golden eyes to look at my appearance and by the look on her face she was impressed with my choice of clothing. I saw her glance at the figure beside me with wide eyes.

"Alice! Where have you been? Esme was so worried about you!" Rosalie said with concern for her sister."I'm fine Rose, just surprised at your visit" Alice replied to the blonde beauty.

"Well Emmett and I have had enough of golden boy and his depressed act... I mean all you hear is 'Bella this' and 'Bella that' it's driving me insane. So I decided I would come and apologise to Bella for leaving..." she trailed off turning her gaze towards me.

"I'm so sorry Bella for being a bitch to you! I didn't mean any of it, I-I..... I just wanted to protect you from our world and I knew I came off as a mean person but I was wondering if you would forgive us and allow us to stay with you? Please..." Rosalie begged. My eyes were wide with shock at the words coming from Rosalie's mouth.

"Um... Yeah, I forgive you Rosalie" I said still a little shocked. She smiled and gently pulled me into a sisterly hug.

"Call me Rose, sis" she whispered in my ear. She slowly withdrew from the hug and I smiled at her. I felt myself being lifted off of the ground and swung around by strong arms.

"I missed you belly" I heard Emmett's deep voice boom causing people passing by to stare. I giggled at Emmett's immaturity.

"I missed you too bro" I replied hugging him tightly. I heard his booming laugh before being settled back down on my feet. I turned to Angela who was standing on the other side of the car watching us with a smile on her face, I signaled her to join us.

'I wonder what they were talking about? I wouldn't want to intrude' I listened into her thoughts

'Is that an Audi r8' I heard rose gawk at my car.

"Rose if you would like you can drive it home this afternoon?" I asked referring to the car. Her eyes lit up with joy.

"Really?" she asked in excitement.

"Sure" I said.

" We better get inside it's going to rain in around a minute" I predicted and checked to see if my prediction was right, which it was.

We made our way to the entry of the old school and entered into the empty hall ways. Just as the door closed it started to rain causing all the students to rush inside. I heard Rose gasp behind me as my prediction was spot on.

"How did she know?" I heard her whisper to Emmett quietly.

"I'm a witch but I'll explain more on that later, the bells going to ring in 3 seconds" I said to the shocked blonde beauty.

"3...2...1" I said as the shrill sound of the school bell resounded in my ears."Come on" I said to Alice since she was in all my classes.

"See you at lunch" I yelled over my shoulder as we walked away towards our first class.

*** Lunch ***

Alice and I waited by the door of the cafeteria waiting for the others to arrive. I saw Rose and Emmett with Angela not far behind.

"Let's enter in style" I suggested giggling. I heard them laugh and nod.

"Ok, Alice and Ange flank me and Rose and Emmett you can walk in after" I planned our entrance. They all nodded, smiling at the idea.

"Let's go!" I shouted and strut in with Ally and Ange flanking me. We laughed as everyone stared and grabbed our trays of food. We gracefully walked towards the furthest table from the staring students.

"You've changed a lot bells not that I don't like it" Emmett said smiling. I smiled back as we sat down.

"Yes I have" I replied sitting between Alice and Rose, Angela was beside Alice and Emmett beside Rose with his arm around her slender waist.

"Never knew you had a stomach like that" Rose stated staring at my outfit.

"I guess eating healthier gets rid of unwanted fat" I replied smiling and glancing down at my toned stomach.

"So apart from us leaving what else have we missed the past few days?" Emmett wondered. I sighed and looked at my big brother.

"Surprisingly a lot, I killed Victoria, found out I was a witch, looked after Alice, met Taylor Swift and got offered a singing career, found out the Volturi are after Alice and I, had a vision of Jane arriving this afternoon and then you guys arrived" I exclaimed. They looked shocked at all the events that had occurred.

"Wow" Emmett boomed.

I nodded and started talking and explaining about the days that had passed.

The day went by fast and soon enough it was time to head home. I leaned against my baby after getting through the crowd of students surrounding the car. I saw Rosalie, Alice and Angela pushing through the crowd of staring students. I handed Rose the keys and she smiled. I winked back and slid into the passenger side.

"Where's Emmett?" I asked once everyone was in.

"He had to take the jeep" Rose explained. I nodded and the car purred to life and Rose swerved out of the parking lot and raced towards Angela's house. I didn't tell her to slow down and just enjoyed the adrenaline pumping through me from the speed. We came to a halt in front of Angela's house she jumped out, laid on the grass and started kissing the ground. We all laughed at the funny act.

"I'm not that bad of a driver" Rose said still giggling at Angela's act.

"Of course not, I enjoyed it!" I exclaimed still laughing.

"Bye Angela, I'll call you if anything happens in training this afternoon" I lied. I couldn't tell her about Jane or the Volturi but I would tell her some of the powers I had found, that is if I have anymore.

"Bye guys" she said as she walked up to her door.

"Time for witch training" I whispered dreading the accounter with the evil blonde girl with devil red eyes.

*****************************Hey guys sorry I haven't updated, I just didn't know what to write for a while plus I had a few exams and assignments take place but I know that I should update more and I will try. Hope you readers liked it!

Like,Comment,Follow &SuggestXOXO Meg

Authors Note

I am sooo sorry! My Wattpad account hasn't been working for a long time. Every time I tried to open it the app it would close again. Soo after a while of playing the waiting game I had to delete then re-download. I am soo sorry! I hope to be updating soon! Thank you!

XOXO Meg

Authors Note part 2

S orry readers not an update! I just wanted to say that I went back and added media in each of my chapters so please check that out and I will update soon! Please don't be afraid to suggest future events or inbox me your name and who you wish to be in the story. You can also suggest future events that can appear in the group just inbox me!

Vote,Comment &SUGGEST

Chapter 19 Training And The Volturi

H ey guys here is chapter 19! I hope you enjoy it!

Disclaimer: I don't own twilight or any of the songs featured in this chapter. :(

Chapter 19- Training and The Volturi

I entered the house with Rose and Alice following. Emmett was exiting his Jeep and would join us in the living room soon. I sunk into the leather couch next to Renee as Rosalie and Alice took a seat on the floor in front of us with Emmett now on the recliner.

"Okay, I have witch training that needs to be completed and Alice and I are expecting a little visitor so we need to make a plan" I proposed to the group. I saw Renee look at Rose and Emmett confused and then at me as I started talking about the visitor.

"I got a vision of Jane coming for a visit. She is from the Volturi, I'm sure you've heard of them mum," I suggested to my mother who nodded along. I could feel Rose and Emmett's confused stares on my face.

"Mum this is Rose and Emmett they are the adoptive brother and sister of Alice, they are also vampires as you could probably tell and will be staying here for a while but I will explain that later as there is more important matters to be discussed. Rose and Emmett this is my mum Renee and she is a witch as well, this is who I got the genes off," I explained so we could move on with the plan.

"Anyway the plan is....."

Time skip

I put my palm up to the sky as my eyes turned white and the sky filled with clouds as small white flecks of cold snowflakes fell from up above. I could sense Rose, Emmett and Renee down wind so Jane wouldn't smell them and they will be there for back up if an attack took place. I controlled the wind to pick up and blow all the snow away and replaced the clouds with sun.

"Why did you stop? I was enjoying the snow" Alice whined like she did in the vision.

"Cold" I repeated what I said in the vision.

"Why don't you use your witch powers and wish for a jumper" she exclaimed in fake annoyance.

"A witch?" I heard the bell like voice come from the forrest as expected. In the blink of an eye Alice was in front of me in a protective crouch. I heard the slight warning growl in the back of her throat.

"What do you want Jane?" I asked her with aggression in my voice. I could feel Renee, Emmett and Rosalie tense getting ready to attack if needed.

"Well I'm here to check on the Cullen Coven and just happened to find little miss Alice's scent so I followed. I'm here to tell you that Master

Aro is having a ball to celebrate his new Volturi member and has invited your coven. Bring your witch friend here along, I'm sure Aro will find her interesting. I'll see you then, pass on the invitation to the rest of your coven. Now that I have done my job I will be on my way. Aro shall know of her and she must show at the ball,in three days" she finished and handed us a fancy invitation.

"Bye cullen, witch" she nodded her head at us before disappearing into the forrest. Renee, Emmett and Rosalie walked into the meadow whilst I opened the fancy piece of paper.

Paper:

Dear Cullen Coven,You are invited to the grand ball I am throwing to welcome a new member to the Volturi. You are welcome to come early but the ball is taking place on the 21st of September. There are guest bedrooms available in the castle for your leisure. The ball starts at 6 and drinks will be available for any diet you choose to live by. We hope to see you there extend this invitation to others.

Aro

The note was written in neat elegant writing, I passed the invitation to the others for them to read. I knew we would need to start to get ready to leave soon.

***********************************Here's Chapter 19 readers. Hope you en-joy!

Vote,Comment,Fan &Suggest

XOXO Meg

Chapter 20 Arival

H ere's chapter 20! Hope you like it! I'm sorry I haven't been updating it is not my creative time and I've been so uninspired plus my friend asked me to cowrite a story with her so go check that out please:

A Sass a day keeps the Basics awayBy Codie Soden.

Disclaimer: I do not own twilight or any of the songs featured in this book. :(

Chapter 20- Arival

I entered the large castle with Alice and Renae beside me and Rosalie and Emmett trailing behind. The sun was rising over the town of Volterra, Italy. It was the day before the grand ball and we somehow convinced Charlie to let us have a "holiday" in Italy. If only he knew how dangerous this trip could turn out to be. I looked towards the gates as I heard footsteps approach.

"I see you brought another witch along master Aro will be pleased Cullens. Where is the rest of your clan?" Jane's taunting voice rang through the hallway as she signaled us to follow.

"We have recently split temporarily due to issues" Rosalie answered not giving to much away.

"Pity" Jane said in fake concern. We continued to make our way down the long tunnel. I shivered as the cold air brushed against my exposed skin. I instantly wished for a jacket, I felt the clothing item appear on my arm and rushed to put the article of clothing on Alice smiled beside me and shook her head.

"Where will we be staying Jane?" Alice asked breaking the silence. We all looked towards the small blonde figure for answers, curious ourselves.

"In the guest rooms, there are others already there" she explained in an emotionless voice but managing to still have the voice of an angel.

"This way" she said signaling us to an elevator. We all stepped in and Jane immediately followed. We all waited patiently for the lift to end, listening to the soft opera music sounding from the small speaker above. A small ding indicated that the lift was over and we proceeded to follow Jane coming into a small lobby.

"Good Morning Signora Jane" a young human woman greeted her behind the front desk, smiling brightly.

"Greta" Jane nodded her greeting towards the woman with a small smile.

"Felix open the doors" Jane commanded as we made our way to two enormous wooden doors. The doors immediately opened and our group stepped through into the room on the other side.

I was amazed at how appointed this space was. The room was very big and some Sunlight Rays were seeping through the huge dome window above us. The circular room had a high ceiling with ancient designs, long poles made an inner circle around the room supporting the structured roof. There was marble flooring and steps that lead up to three beautifully designed thrones, each one holding a figure. I stared at the beautiful creatures that sat on these thrones and instantly recognized them as Aro, Marcus and Caius the gods from the painting in Carlisle's office. Jane bowed her head and looked at the three rulers.

"This is the witch I was informing you of Master she has bought a friend of hers along. They are with half of the Cullen clan, as the other half could not join us" She explained to the middle man with Black shoulder length hair and red eyes who I assumed was Aro. He nodded smiling at the blonde before casting his eyes on our group. I glanced at the other two figures, who I am assuming are Marcus with the long dark brown hair and Caius with the shoulder length blonde almost white hair.

"Where are the other Cullens?" He asked out of curiosity. I took a small step forward and took a breathe.

"We have recently split ways with the others of the Cullen clan as some issues have arisen that need to be faced before the reunion of this clan" I explained the current circumstances.

"And you must be the witch. Am I right?" He said with a smile on his face

.

"Yes you are not mistaken and this is my mother" I explained the presence of the other witch.

"When did you um... evolve?" He said trying to find the right word. I swallowed not liking the idea of giving away to much information but I knew I had to.

"Only a few days ago, after my eighteenth birthday" I responded. I felt Renae join me by my side.

"I changed years ago, a few days after my eighteenth birthday as well" Renae said as she looked at the man before us.

"Could you demonstrate some of your powers, the younger one" Aro said getting excited. I nodded and glanced at the group behind us.

"You may want to move back" I said to them. As soon as the words left my mouth everyone moved to the walls of the room.

I walked to the middle and closed my eyes taking a deep breathe. I imagined a tornado wrapping around me and instantly felt the wind gust around me I didn't make it very strong as I didn't want to upset them by wrecking their castle. I imagined myself levitating above the ground the wind still gusting around me. I felt my feet leave the ground and heard a few people gasp. I started to spin giving them a show to remember, I made the wind stop and gently placed myself on the ground. I knew they wanted more so I stuck out my hands with my palms facing upwards and imagined fire on one and ice on the other I opened my eyes and smiled as I saw the bright flame on my left hand and the ice sculpture on the other. I let them disappear from my hands and turned towards Alice and signaled her forward. She appeared in front of me in a flash smiling at me.

"Okay Alice I'm going to try compel you but don't worry I won't make you do anything embarrassing. Can you trust me to be in control of your mind for a moment?" I asked hoping this would work. She nodded her confirmation and smiled encouraging me to continue. I stared into her Golden eyes as she stared back into mine.

"I command you to do as I say" I said going on gut instinct as I clicked my fingers and Alice went into a trance.

"Yes master Bella" She said staring at me waiting for my command . I smiled at my success as I heard gasps and whispers behind me.

"I want you to do a lap of the room and return back here as fast as you can and then I would like you to do that again but at a human slow jogging rate" I commanded the small pixie. At the speed of lightning she was back in front of me after doing a fast lap of the throne room. She then proceeded to do a slow human jog of the room I took this time to glance around the room and saw everyone staring at either me or Alice shocked even Renae was overwhelmed. As soon as Alice was back in front of me I stepped forward and stared into her eyes again.

"I release my command over you" I said on gut instinct again and snapped my fingers. Suddenly Alice shook her head coming back from the trance.

"What happened Bells? Have you compelled me yet?" She exclaimed confused.

"Yes, it's over now Alice. You must not remember anything" I said as I hugged her then pushed her away gently whilst signaling that I was finished by bowing towards everyone. Instantly I was surrounded by Renae and the other Cullens again. I smiled as I hugged my mother with her whispering how proud she was in my ear. I had Emmett bear hug me next telling me how awesome it was. I felt Rosalie gently take me into her arms nothing like her husband and congratulated me on my achievements. I grabbed Alice's hand and stepped out from the group looking at the three awestruck leaders. They really aren't as scary as Edward described, they were actually quite polite and considerate.

"That was amazing dear. What is your name young one?" He said as he walked gracefully towards me.

"Isabella Swan but I prefer Bella" I said as I watched his elegant descent with Marcus on his right and Caius on his left.

"And may I ask your mothers name?" He exclaimed politely with a friendly grin on his face.

"Renae Swan" I responded as I glanced at my mother she smiled as we locked eyes for a second.

"Well such talented witches like you two definitely deserve a spot in the Volturi" He said as he stood before me offering a proposal. I glanced at my mother who slightly shook her head.

"It would be an honor but we do have lives we need to get back to and for my case a coven to return to" I said glancing at the ones surrounding me. "But I would offer my help and loyalty if needed for a mission or a fight at any time. In return that my mother is left to live her life" I offered the leader. He smiled excited at my proposal.

"Most definitely, I accept your offer that means you are now officially a part of the Volturi . If we need any help I will send someone to inform you. Jane, you know what to do to welcome new members" he said and Jane disappeared from the room and reappeared with two items in her hand.

I stepped forward releasing Alice's hand as I did so. Aro grabbed the first item from Jane's hand which appeared to be a jewelry box. He opened the box and nestled inside lay the crest that reside around each of their necks hanging by a chain. He flashed behind me and linked the necklace behind my neck before returning to his ordinal place. He then proceeded to grab the black clothing item from Jane's hand and unraveled the neatly folded item to reveal a long black cloak, the same that Jane was wearing. I smiled at the welcome and allowed him to put it on over my black long sleeved t-shirt with intricate swirl designs and my designer skinny jeans, I was also wearing high Black pumps with my hair down and slight make up. He clapped excitingly seeing his new member accepting the welcome even though I wasn't going to stay in the castle with them I still felt excited to be a part of something so special.

"Okay, well now that the welcome is done we should probably get you guest to your room. Once your settled meet back down here so I can introduce everyone" he exclaimed still excited about the recent exchange.

He signaled a young boy to take us. "This is Alec, Jane's twin brother he will take you to your rooms"

We followed the young boy as he made his way through the tunnels. I memorized the way as we went so I didn't get lost on the way back to the throne room. He stopped in front of two doors opposite each other and another two could be seen down the hallway a bit.

"These three rooms are yours I assume you would like to split yourselves up. The kitchen is down the hall third door to your left and the entertainment room is opposite that with the music, art room and library in the doors after those. So get yourselves settled in, there is one double bed in every room so four of you will have to share a bed with another guest and one will have a double to their self. Although most of you don't sleep anyway. If there is a problem though please inform us in the throne room" he explained before bowing his head and smiling as he walked away. I turned towards the group.

"Rosalie and Emmett room 1, Alice and I room 2 and mum can have room 3. Sound good?" I asked the group they all nodded smiling at the arrangements. I linked arms with Alice as I opened the room door we both gasped as we took in the room we were staying in. I smiled at Alice as we heard someone coming down the hallway and we both glanced outside as a man placed our luggage in front of us.

"Thank you" I said in gratitude towards the man. He smiled and proceeded to drop off the others luggage as well. I grabbed mine and placed it next to the bed to unpack later.

I examined the huge room in amazement. The room had a big king sized bed with golden covers that had swirl designs in black and more pillows than two people would need. The carpet was a light golden brown colour matching the walls with a white ceiling that held a small chandelier hanging from a chain. The room was fully furnished with ancient timber draws and vanities and other pieces of furniture. There was a leather couch that looked comfortable facing a huge TV hung on the wall.

I cast my eyes to the huge window that took up a little less than half of the furthest wall. I could see the city and the sun was rising further into the sky, there was a small balcony with two chairs and a small circular table. I could see two doors in the room and instantly my curiosity spiked I opened the closest door to me on the wall to my left. It was a large ensuite with a shower that could fit two inside and a long vanity with a sink and mirror for make up and other toiletries. I closed that door and entered the one next to it to find Alice unpacking both our luggage into the huge walk in closet. She turned as I entered and grinned at my awestruck expression.

"The room is amazing isn't it?" She said as she hung up both of our ball dresses. I smiled and nodded my agreement sitting down on the seat in the middle of the clothing racks.

"About joining the Volturi congratulations. I wouldn't think clumsy Bella Swan, would be protecting the Vampire world" She teased as she laughed at her own joke. I playfully glared at her as I tried not to laugh myself.

"I've become rather graceful lately and I haven't tripped once yet today in these killer heels" I said lifting up my feet to display them. She laughed and continued to unpack our belongings. I decided to have a shower and get changed so I could get rid of all the grime from the flight and my 'little show'. I grabbed a black long sleeved crop top and black ripped skinny jeans and my black flats.

After my shower I got dressed and grabbed my newly acquired cloak. I decided to go down to the throne room, singing softly along the way, and talk to my new masters and fellow guard members.

I said goodbye to Alice who was sorting out the make up for tomorrow night, she responded with a smile and continued on with her task. I made my way down the twisting tunnels and followed the path that I had memorized. I reached the large double doors getting excited but that excitement was short lived when I heard the voice on the other side of the door. I froze and instantly I felt anger and sadness boil up inside of me. I slammed the doors open to see 5 figures in front of me confirming my fear. I knew what I had to do as soon as I saw HIS face turn my way. Karma is going to hurt....

****

Long chapter for you hopefully making it up to you readers for my writers block. I would love you to check out the book I am co writing it is in my reading list "co-written stories" if you can't find it. It is called "A Sass A Day Keeps The Basics Away" by Codie Soden. Thanks for supporting me guys!

Vote,Comment, Suggest &Follow

XOXO Meg

Chapter 21 Holding Back

- -

Hey guys! Here's another chapter for you readers! I hope you enjoy!

Disclaimer: I do not own twilight or any of the songs featured in this chapter. :(

Chapter 21- Holding Back

I flashed over the other side of the room trying to calm down as I sat on the top step in front of my new masters. I saw all of them staring at me shocked at my presence especially the crest around my neck and the cloak. Aro smiled approaching me and pulling me into a gentle hug that I wasn't expecting.

"Master Aro, I came to greet my fellow guard members" I said ignoring the figures behind me still feeling their gazes bore into my back.

"Well of course, I will just finish up business here before we start, feel free to take a seat in my throne" he said in a gentle friendly voice. I was really starting to like Aro and knew he would be like a father to me in time. I sat down on his throne, crossing my legs and trying to keep my mind distracted so I wouldn't go on a rampage and kill HIM in front of everyone. I sighed deeply as I leant back into the big throne. I stared at the other part of the Cullen clan and immediately glared at HIS shocked face. I could see that Esme and Carlisle were just as shocked whilst Jasper and who I assume was his mate were more calm.

"Bella?" He asked in disbelief as he blinked rapidly and took a step forward. I growled at the sound of his voice and glared at him with cold eyes. I turned to a confused Aro, who was glancing between us in confusion. I knew of his power and signaled him towards me.

"I will show you later. I'll take them to their room if your finished here Master" I volunteered. He nodded as he glanced at Edward, I thought his name in disgust. I rose from the throne and descended the marble steps towards them with every eye following my movements.

"Follow me and DON'T try anything" I said in a threatening voice as I walked towards the double doors.

"Jane will you join us and lead us to where the Cullens will be staying" I said politely to the young blonde. She nodded leading the way through the tunnels as I didn't know where they were staying.

"Bella could you lead the single one to the spare room near your bedroom. I will take the rest as they are in the rooms before you" I nodded clenching my jaw as I followed orders.

"Yes, Jane. Follow me Edward" I commanded. I felt him follow after my quick steps.

"Bella I-" he uttered before I interrupted him.

"Don't want to hear it Edward! Leave me alone and don't try anything!" I commanded as I walked faster I was getting closer to our destination and I could finally leave and not have his company.

"But-" he exclaimed. I turned around and glared at him interrupting him again.

"I said don't and I should not need to repeat myself. I am not the wimpy little Bella you left behind in Forks and I am not afraid of killing you in fact I am holding myself back not to kill you so don't push it. Am I clear Edward?" I ask as I spat his name in disgust. He tilted his head confused by my words.

"But your still human" he said as he took a step forward in return to me stepping back.

"And that is where you are mistaken" I said as I turned around and continued walking I heard him pause for a minute before running to catch up.

"What do you mean your not human?" He asked. I turned around closing my eyes and reached out my hand imagining him pressed against the wall with his feet off the ground. I opened my eyes to see him struggling against the wall as I paced in front of him glaring menacingly at him.

"I don't need to answer to you anymore. I have changed, I am more confident now Edward. I know what I want now and you are not going to be a part of my life any more. So before you get killed, think of what you are doing and LEAVE ME ALONE!" I threatened in a scary voice. He gulped and nodded before I released him. He fell to the ground panting and out of breathe I glared at him before giving him my hand. He hesitated before taking the offer, I pulled him up a little to hard which earned me a groan.

"Don't test me Edward because it will be worse next time" I whispered as I released his hand and turned towards the tunnels again.

"Bella! Are you alright? I heard a commotion..." Alice trailed off seeing who was panting with his hands on his knees behind us. I saw her take a step forward ready to attack but I grabbed her arm and looked into her eyes telling her not to.

"I think he knows to leave me alone. I already taught him not to question me" I said as I linked arms with her. She still looked stiff ready to attack at any moment but she softened at my reassurance. I began to walk towards the room and heard Edward follow behind with caution.

"So are we set up for the ball tomorrow Alice?" I asked distracting her and myself from the figure following behind us. She nodded and glanced behind us casting a glare at her 'brother'.

"Are you ready to be welcomed by your new coven?" She asked in return. I nodded not wanting to give too much away with him listening.

"I am looking forward to finding out more about myself and what I am capable of. I already know I can defeat a Vampire at least" I explained wording my answer in a way that doesn't reveal too much. We arrived at the door opposite my mothers. She exited the room curious to see the presences outside her door.

"Bella is everything alright?" She asked in concern. Looking at Edward curiously not recognizing him.

"Yes mum just showing the guest where he is staying" I explained. I gestured Edward to his room.

"Your luggage should be here soon. Make your self at home" I said wanting to leave I turned but half way through he grabbed my arm.

"Bella" he said. I turned and glared at his hand that was around my upper arm, he immediately let it go taking a step forward as I stepped back. I felt Alice stiffen and stand beside me glaring at her 'brother', Renae was confused about the commotion and started to get a bit defensive over her daughter.

"Who gave you the right to speak to me. I am going to make my self nice and clear, leave.me.alone.Edward" I commanded. At the sound of his name a look of recognition came across Renae's face. Instantly Edward was on the ground grabbing his head in pain.

"So you were the one that left my daughter that made her suffer. You deserve to suffer after what you did to my daughter" she said fiercely as she glared at the man I had loved long ago. He screamed as the pain seemed to get worse.

"Mum, he isn't worth it" I said calmly emphasizing each word. She concentrated harder, I walked towards her and placed my hand on her shoulder.

"Mum, stop" I commanded as I said she released him and turned to me with concern.

"I'm fine mum, seriously" I reassured her as I rubbed her arm and hugged her before telling her to go back into her room. She nodded complying but not before giving Edward one more moment of pain. I shook my head and turned towards Alice grabbing her hand as I started to walk away.

"I hope you learned your lesson Edward" I exclaimed over my shoulder getting a groan in response. I turned towards Alice "We're done here"

I walked faster towards the throne room with Alice on my arm.

"Come on I have to talk to Aro" I said as I used super speed to reach my destination faster. I appeared in front of the doors in seconds with Alice appearing not long after.

"Open the doors please" I requested. The doors opened and I strut in towards Master Aro. I bowed my head to all three rulers and walked gracefully up the stairs as Aro stood to greet me with another welcoming hug.

"Are you alright my dear? You seem a little stiff and defensive" he said in concern, pure sincerity in his red eyes. I nodded and took a deep breathe a plan forming in my mind on how to explain my past to the rulers of the Vampire world.

"I am going to link my mind with yours and Master Marcus and Caius to show you my past and explain the relation between Edward and I. If that is alright?" I asked permission to enter their minds. Aro nodded curious to see what I had to show, glancing at his brothers who also nodded their acceptance. I closed my eyes and connected to their minds channelling their brain. I then proceeded to display my thoughts, sights and feelings starting from my move to forks up until a few minutes ago. I released my hold on their minds and heard them all gasp and look at me amazed.

"I'm so sorry my dear Isabella. I know you wouldn't want us to kill him even though I'm sure we all do after seeing how he left you but we will hold back" he said pulling me into a soft hug. I willed myself not to cry and show weakness but one traitor tear fell which I quickly wiped away before anyone could see. I smiled as I released from the hug and was pulled into another from Marcus, even Caius.

"Well now we should probably introduce the other coven members" Aro exclaimed as he made a call and suddenly lots of Vampires filled the room.

"This is Isabella Swan our new member but she prefers Bella. She is a very powerful witch so treat her right and welcome her to the family" Caius said throwing in the small warning not to mess with me making me smile in his direction to which he returned with his own. The guard made a line waiting to meet the new member. I just couldn't wait until I was officially a part of this coven.

****

Hey guys two long chapters in one day! Hopefully to make it up to you readers! Hope you enjoyed this chapter and don't be afraid to suggest possible plot lines or twist as I am open to suggestions within reason of course. So message me your suggestions or request. There's more chapters to come so stay tuned!

Vote,Comment,Suggest &Follow

XOXO Meg

Chapter 22 True Potential

Hey guys here's chapter 22! Hope you like it! Got some more of Bella's powers revealed in this chapter!

Disclaimer: I do not own twilight or any of the songs featured in this story.

Chapter 22- True Potential

All the guard members came up one by one and politely introduced themselves. I shook hands with each individual getting used to the cold hands placed in mine. Once the introductions were made Aro clapped his pale hands earning everyone's attention.

"That is all my darlings, you are dismissed" he said smiling. At his words the guards disappeared going back to where they were before. I turned to the three masters as Alice grabbed my hand and I smiled at her.

"Dear Bella would you care to follow me to the training room as I would like to see some of your other powers to see your true potential" Aro explained signaling me to follow as he exited the door. I looked to Alice questioning if she'd like to join, she nodded and linked arms with me. I strut after Aro following his path as we walked through the endless tunnels. I memorized the way as we approached a large door.

Aro gestured us to enter first, we entered the huge room and I instantly gasped. The room was made from some type of stone that looked hard to break, there was seats situated all around the outside of the room for spectators. In the center of the enormous room stood two figures as we grew closer I recognized them as Demetri and Felix from the introductions made before.

"Master and Bella" they greeted at the same time. I nodded at the two fellow guard members.

"Felix, Demetri. Bella here has come to train could you show her to the change room I have ordered Jane to get Bella an outfit so it should be in there" Aro ordered before taking a seat on one of the benches surrounding the room. Alice followed me to the changing rooms following after the two guard members. I opened the door and smiled at the two in gratitude as I pulled Alice into the room and closed the door.

I changed into the outfit that was laid out in front of me. It was a black singlet and a long sleeved black top made from a strong material accompanied with tights made from the same material. I must say I looked hot. I laughed when I saw Alice had closed her eyes to give me privacy.

"You can open your eyes now Ally" I whispered as I laughed some more. She slowly opened her eyelids to reveal the butterscotch eyes they held. I grabbed her hand and dragged her from the room and into the training room. I forced her to sit at the bench next to Aro as I approached the middle of the floor ready for any command.

"Felix I need you to go up against Bella so I can see if she can take an experienced vampire attacker. Do not hurt her though" Aro commanded as Felix rose from his place on the bench next to Demetri.

"Yes master" he responded as he got into a defensive crouch in front of me.

"Bella are you ready" Aro asked as I nodded in response "go"

I stayed in place as Felix ran at me full speed, at the last minute I imagined a bubble around me that allowed no one to pass through. As Felix reached the bubble he immediately bounced back and fell to the floor before he could get back up I imagined unbreakable chains wrapped around his body keeping him to the ground he struggled trying to break free. I was going on instinct the whole time I slowly approached Felix and twisted my finger pointing at his head. Suddenly his screams were heard in the room, I stopped once I heard Aro clap earning my attention.

"Well done dear Bella now I would like to see you deal with more than one attacker so would you release Felix now dear" He commanded in a sweet tone clearly impressed I nodded and released the chains from Felix's body. I offered him my hand which he took and I helped him up as I smiled at him apologetic for my actions to which he nodded. I moved back to my previous place across the room as Demetri joined Felix.

"Jane and Alec" Aro called and the twins flashed into the room "would you do the honor of fighting Bella with Felix and Demetri?" He asked the duo.

They nodded and the four made a circle surrounding me. I instantly put up the physical shield in a bubble but this time I made it like a second skin so I could fight but not be hurt. I nodded to Aro signaling I was ready.

"Go" Aro commanded. I felt Jane attempting to use her power on me to no avail. I saw a black mist seep towards me slowly coming from Alec's hands. I turned to see Felix and Demetri waiting for the powers to take place before any attack took place. The mist reached me and I didn't feel any different. I heard Aro gasp and instantly he spoke up.

"Dearest Bella how come the powers are not affecting you?" He asked curiously.

"I have what I refer to as a mental shield no powers work on me as my mind is repelling them" I explained as I watched the mist retreat and Jane stopped using her power knowing it was no use. I saw them all getting into a crouch ready to attack all at the same time. I heard Demetri start to bolt towards me but after the first few steps I had paralyzed him and prepared for the next move. I heard Jane take a step forward and then another before I turned and pointed a finger at her head and she dropped to the ground in pain which I released as I felt bad. Instead I created a invisible barrier around her so she was stuck inside. I saw Alec and Felix nod at each other before attacking at the same time. I surrounded Felix with a ring of fire and I teleported out of the way of Alec's attack before making him paralyzed, using his own power against him as I had to Jane. I heard Aro clap again after realising that I had won again. I released the four guards from the state they were in and I strut up to Aro as he signaled me over.

"Bella dear I would like to see you protect some people whilst fighting against more guard members so I know that you can both protect and attack at the same time" He explained to me as I nodded agreeing as I hadn't felt tired yet "Good"

He made the same sound that he had made to gather the guard before even Masters Caius and Marcus had come.

"Okay, I need you here as Bella is training and we need the whole guard to attack her all at once to see if she is ready to fight in a battle" He explained to his guard members "Now into your battle positions" He commanded.

They all got into formation on the other side of the room the three masters stood behind me with Aro feeling confident that I could protect them. Alice joined them on Aro's command. I saw some guest enter the room curious on what was happening as they took a seat. I saw the Cullens enter and I glared at HIM. Emmett and Rosalie walked up to me and stood beside me looking curious as to what is going on. I heard Alice explain it to them and they nodded looking wary if I could take the entire guard. They fell into place behind me in support. Once it looked like everything had been prepared I raised the physical shield to surround them and made sure they couldn't get out to help me incase they decided play hero and get hurt. I raised one around myself so no one could come within a meter of me. I nodded to Aro indicating I was ready.

"Go!" Aro commanded the guard to attack they all proceeded to run full speed towards me. I raised my hands towards them and instantly half of them were paralyzed I then twisted my finger pointing to the rest and they all dropped to the ground grasping their heads in pain. I felt guilty again and released them then wrap each individual in vines holding them in place. There was only one left and I realized that she must have been a shield as well. I knew that I couldn't use many of my powers on her because of that fact so I acted on instinct as she ran at me before realizing that she couldn't reach me through the shield placed around me. I held my hand out Palm facing upwards and imagined draining her power and instantly I could see her growing weak and I could tell her shield had dropped I immediately put her into a deep sleep that only I could wake her from. I heard her body drop to the floor and her soft snores could be heard. I turned towards the Masters who were assessing the damage done to their guard with impressed looks. I dropped my shields still not feeling tired. I felt Alice hug me and Rosalie joined as I laughed at the two concerned figures. I high fived Emmett before being pulled into a bear hug.

"Wow bells or should I call you almighty one now?" Emmett teased as he let out a booming laugh. I punched his shoulder lightly and laughed with him before turning to the Masters who had collected themselves. I slowly released the shocked guards from there state and I heard them all gasp looking at me with a new found respect.

"Dearest Bella I am truly glad that you chose to join us even on your conditions. You are truly a talented young lady with a lot of potential.

Would you like to continue training here in the castle after the ball I would love to see you evolve? If so you can visit any time you wish to do so" Aro said with hope in his voice.

"I would be honored Master Aro but I may not visit as often as you like as I am still at school and have other commitments back home waiting for me but I will try to return often" I explained as I smiled. He nodded in understanding seeming glad that I would try to come. I turned towards the guards felling guilty again.

"Sorry guys" I apologized to them. They all nodded smiling at me showing they wouldn't hold it against me. I grinned and turned to Aro again.

"Am I allowed to leave to change and go out to explore Volterra tonight Master Aro?" I asked permission.

"Sure dearest Bella be careful and bring at least two guards with you just incase" He responded. I nodded and he hugged me softly as did Marcus and Caius before I strut to the changing room. I felt Alice and Rosalie enter after me before the door was closed I changed and told Rose and Alice I was ready before exiting the room with them following. The training room had emptied apart from seven figures. I saw Rosalie run up to Emmett and link hands before kissing his cheek.

"Bella, Alec and I have been assigned to stay with you outside of the gates tonight" Jane said as she and her twin flanked Alice and I. I smiled at the two before turning to see the other four figures that remained in the room.

"Bella, we missed you so much honey" Esme exclaimed as she looked at me with such soft and caring eyes. Carlisle wrapped his arm around his wife as if to comfort her.

"The family wasn't the same without you" Carlisle added. I smiled immediately forgiving them knowing it wasn't their fault that their son was like this. I ran up to Esme and enveloped her in a hug as she started to sob quietly into my shoulder.

"I finally got my daughter back" she whispered as she pulled back and kissed my forehead. I felt Carlisle hug me next and I sighed in content.

"I missed you sweetheart" he said into my hair before pulling away. I saw Esme run up to Alice, Rosalie and Emmett and hugged them whispering how worried she was. I saw Carlisle do the same welcoming his children back again. I turned and saw Jasper standing next to a beautiful vampire with long brown locks and golden eyes, I recognized her from Alice's flashback as Jasper's mate. Jasper approached me I twisted my fingers and he went to the ground in pain for a moment before I released him. I earned the attention of everyone in the room.

"It will be worse if you ever hurt my sister again" I said before offering my hand to help him up. I hugged him and he slowly returned the action shocked.

"I'll let it slide this time Jazz and before you apologize for what happened at my birthday don't because it wasn't your fault and I refuse to forgive you if there is nothing to forgive" I whispered in his ear. He shook his head in disagreement to my statement.

"It was my fault that we left, this would never have happened if I hadn't have done that" he said looking down in shame after pulling away from the hug. I grabbed his chin and forced him to look at me.

"No it wasn't your fault Jasper. You not only have to control your own lust, you also have everyone else's on top of that. Everyone thinks you are the weakest in this coven but really your the strongest as you hold back even with everyone else's lust and hunger on top of your own. No vampire in your place at that time could possibly hold back no matter now experienced. So don't be so hard on yourself" I said finishing my rant and I was suddenly crushed to his chest.

"Thank you Bella" he said in gratitude "I never thought of it that way before"

"Your welcome Jazz but I was serious about my warning" I said as I pulled back gently. He gulped nodding as he glanced at Alice who was chatting away to Esme but I could distinctly see her listening to our conversation as her head was tilted this way and she kept glancing at the exchange.

"Now go and apologise while I meet your new mate" I said and he nodded making a bee line for Alice who had stopped her conversation so she was ready. I turned towards his mate and strut towards the new family member. Once I had reached her I outstretched my hand.

"I'm Bella you must be Jasper's new mate" I said as she shook my hand with a friendly smile on her flawless face.

"I'm Ashley, I've heard a lot of things about you" she introduced herself.

"Good things I hope" I exclaimed with a laugh. She nodded laughing alongside me.

"So got any special powers Ashley?" I asked her curiously.

"Yes I can communicate through minds, like telepathy" she explained. I nodded and heard Alice call for me I quickly excused myself and flashed to her side she looked at me and tilted her head towards the door. My head snapped in the direction to see I hadn't noticed HIM standing there staring at me the whole time.

"Edward" I said a strained greeting with my jaw clenched.

"Bella" He whispered back looking at me longingly. I turned towards the others and grabbed Alice's hand.

"We are going to town I will see you when we return" I said to them as I linked arms with Alice and strut to the door to get prepared to go to town I felt Jane and Alec follow after us flanking us again. I passed Edward giving him a glare and growled as he stepped forward causing him to step back again looking ashamed. I got to Alice and I's room and walked into the closet changing into a white lace summer dress and brushed through my hair leaving it to cascade over my shoulder in soft curls I put on a bit of mascara and lip gloss before turning to Alice. She was in a casual golden dress with some gold heels. I placed on some white heels to Alice's delight and grabbed my phone and purse.

I glanced at my phone to see Charlie has called as I had gave him my phone number before our 'vacation'. I decided to ring him back on our way to town. I dialed his number as I exited the room to see Jane and Alec had changed into more casual clothes so there won't be suspicion. I placed the phone to my ear hearing it ring, it stopped after the third ring was heard. Jane started to lead the way as the phone connected to my father.

"Hello Swan residents Charlie speaking" I heard his gruff voice answer.

"Hey dad, it's Bella ringing back did you need something important Dad?" I asked my father figure.

"No,no. Just wondering how the vacation is?" He asked.

"It's great dad we got in this morning and it is beautiful here we have even met a few friends and we are going to there party tomorrow night" I explained. I saw Jane glancing at me curiously obviously overhearing the conversation.

"That's great bells. Um.... I have to ask have you found any new powers yet?" He asked awkwardly not knowing how to approach the subject.

"Yes dad and I promise to show you a few when I get back could you tell Angela for me please. I know she is sad she couldn't join us but she understands why" I said feeling guilty for leaving her there.

"Sure Bells. I better leave you to go have fun I will see you in a few days baby girl take care. Tell Renae I said hi. Love you bells, bye" he said ending the conversation.

"I love you too dad, bye" I exclaimed before hanging up. Alice smiled at me and linked arms with me.

"So where would you like to go Bella" Jane said as she opened a door to reveal a huge garage filled with many different expensive cars, Rosalie would be in heaven.

"The mall please" I requested to which she nodded and jumped into the drivers side of a yellow Porsche. Alice and I got in the back so Alec could have passenger seat.

"The mall it is then" Jane replied as she sped out of the space.

****

Here it is a long chapter for you readers! Hope you like it! There is some singing to come in the next chapter! Thinking about changing the summary what do you think leave it in the comments below or even message me a new one!

Vote,Comment, Follow & Suggest

XOXO Meg

Chapter 23 Karaoke Night

Hey guys here's chapter 23! Hope you enjoy! Sorry I haven't updated in a long time between having two weeks without Internet on a cruise ship and coming back to a stack of assignments and exams I've been really busy! Anyway enjoy!

Disclaimer: I do not own twilight or any of the songs featured in this book.

Chapter 23- Karaoke Night

I exited the flashy car and linked arms with Alice as we made our path to the entrance of the mall with Jane and Alec flanking us. The mall was big and looked like it held numerous shops and restaurants. My stomach growled thinking about food and I realised I didn't have lunch or breakfast.

"Better feed your inner monster there Izzy" Alice said using my nickname which earned confused stares from Jane and Alec. I blushed slightly and laughed nodding wholeheartedly in agreement.

"I really want Pizza" I complained to the pixie. Alice grinned and started pulling me in what I assumed was the direction of a pizza place. Once we reached our destination I saw a Italian restaurant with a sign that read

'Karaoke Night' out the front. I glanced at Alice suspiciously knowing why she chose this particular restaurant.

"Oh look Bella! What a coincidence! It's karaoke night, why don't you sing a song or two" Alice said with a cheeky grin. I glared playfully at the pixie knowing that she set this up.

Stupid Future Seeing Pixie

I sighed and nodded giving in as a waiter showed us to a table for four. I sat down and picked up the song menu that the waiter gave us. I glanced over the long list of music and decided which song I was going to perform for the small crowd. I told Alice my food preference incase the waiter came by when I was on stage. I strut up to the DJ next to the stage and he handed me a microphone and I told him which song I would like. He started looking for the song on his laptop and nodded signaling he had it prepared. I walked on stage and brought the mic to my lips as I glanced at Alice to see she was recording me on my phone and Jane on her phone. I slightly shook my head before taking a deep breath.

"Hey guys, I'm Bella and I'll be singing Warrior by Demi Lovato" I said as I nodded at the DJ to start the music.

"This is a story that I have never toldI gotta get this off my chest to let it goI need to take back the light inside you stoleYou're a criminalAnd you steal like you're a pro

All the pain and the truthI wear like a battle woundSo ashamed, so confusedI was broken and bruised

Now I'm a warriorNow I've got thicker skinI'm a warriorI'm stronger than I've ever beenAnd my armor, is made of steel, you can't get inI'm a warriorAnd you can never hurt me again

Out of the ashes, I'm burning like a fireYou can save your apologies, you're nothing but a liarI've got shame, I've got scarsThat I will never showI'm a survivorIn more ways than you know

Cause all the pain and the truthI wear like a battle woundSo ashamed, so confusedI'm not broken or bruised

'Cause now I'm a warriorNow I've got thicker skinI'm a warriorI'm stronger than I've ever beenAnd my armor, is made of steel, you can't get inI'm a warriorAnd you can never hurt me

There's a part of me I can't get backA little girl grew up too fastAll it took was once, I'll never be the sameNow I'm taking back my life todayNothing left that you can sayCause you are never gonna take the blame anyway

Now I'm a warriorI've got thicker skinI'm a warriorI'm stronger than I've ever beenAnd my armor, is made of steel, you can't get inI'm a warriorAnd you can never hurt me again

No oh, yeah, yeah

You can never hurt me again"

I finished the final note in perfect harmony. I looked around the crowd and saw tears in everyone's eyes before they all started clapping. I saw Alice beaming proudly at me and Jane and Alec looked surprised.

"Thank you so much" I said as I exited the stage and handed the smiling DJ the microphone back before walking gracefully back to the table to find my pizza waiting. I smiled at my companions before sitting down and digging in. I was finished the whole pizza in no time. What can I say I was starving. Once I had finished I glanced at the time to see it was 5 o'clock.

"Come on pixie, I assume you want to go to a few shops before we leave to go explore somewhere else" I said as I got up and grabbed money from my purse to pay for the pizza leaving a generous tip. I felt Alice link arms with me as Jane and Alec followed behind. Alice was bouncing in excitement.

"Now, now Alice don't get too excited you might spontaneously combust" I exclaimed laughing as the pixie grimaced at me. She started to pull me into a fancy looking store and forced me to try on everything that she handed me. Jane and Alec watched in amusement grateful it wasn't them in my place. After various different stores we decided to leave and go someplace else. I had collected two new dresses, two new pairs of pants, one pair of shorts, two jumpers and two new shirts. I gladly entered the safety of the car ready for the next place before traveling back to the castle. Alice got in with me and her twenty two shopping bags. I laughed at the amount of clothes she had brought shaking my head at the small shopaholic.

"What some are for Rosalie and Esme as well" She explained the large amount of bags in her hand. It was now 6:45 and we decided to head to the boating docks to walk along the side walk and the small beach.

~~~~~time skip~~~~~~

I walked along the beach carrying my heels feeling the soft sand beneath my toes. My free arm was thread through Alice's as the two guards followed after us. I looked at the moon beaming down on us from above. I felt at ease and relaxed as I spotted a small cafe up the beach. I tugged Alice in the direction wanting some coffee and possibly some Ice-Cream. I entered the small cafe and instantly the smell of fresh coffee hit my taste buds making my mouth water. I quickly strut up to the counter towards a older lady situated behind it.

"Hi, um could I get a Black Coffee with two sugars and a chocolate sundae please" I requested as the lady wrote down my order on the small paper pad nodding.
~~~~~

"That will be $6.50 please" she said in an Italian accent. I handed her the required money and took a seat at a table with four seats as I waited with the others.

"I don't see you having coffee very often" I heard Alice say giggling slightly.

"What can I say I am craving it at the moment plus I need the energy since Vampires don't sleep" I whispered and laughed making sure the very few customers didn't hear me. She joined in and I could hear Jane and Alec snicker trying to hide their smiles.

"You can laugh if you want. Loosen up a little would ya? Stop being so serious" I said as I grinned punching Alec softly on the arm. They both grinned and softly chuckled at me telling them what to do.

"Here you go hon, will that be everything" the same lady placed my food in front of me.

"Yes, thank you" I said as I started to eat my Ice-Cream in glee. I heard her walk away to serve another customer. I took a sip of my coffee and moaned at the taste in my mouth. I heard Alice and the twins laughing softly at my expense. I playfully glared before grinning and finishing my food in record timing. Before I knew it we were back in the car speeding back to the castle. I closed my eyes and sighed as I knew I would have to explain everything to the Cullens when I return including how I could defeat the whole guard. I felt Alice rub my shoulder and I opened my eyes to see we had arrived I exited the car and linked arms with Alice dismissing the two guards with a smile. I turned to Alice grinning at the small pixie.

"I'm going to teleport to our room. Want to join me?" I said as I offered my hand. She nodded grinning at my proposal before grabbing my hand in complete confidence in my ability. I imagined our room in my mind and willed myself to transport Alice and myself to the destination in my mind. In seconds we both appeared in the large room.

"I need to change into something more comfortable and less revealing so I don't have to worry about tempting Edward" I said his name in disgust as I opened the large closets doors searching for an outfit. I couldn't find any that suited the occasion making me growl in frustration before it dawned on me.

"Idiot" I whispered to myself as I realised I just had to imagine the clothes I wanted and then use my powers to get them. I put the image of the clothes I desired and instantly I felt the material replace my white dress and heels. I glanced over my outfit and walked out of the closet feeling more comfortable in my attire. I saw Alice having the same problem and immediately grabbed her shoulders telling her to slow down.

"Let me help with that. Now do as I say; close your eyes and imagine the outfit you want and I will do the rest" I explained. She turned towards me and instantly relaxed closing her eyes. I entered her mind to see what she wanted and immediately complied. She gasped as she felt the fabric replace the dress and heels that was there before. She opened her eyes and gaped as she assessed her outfit. She squealed and hugged me excited to know that she could have any outfit she wanted at any time with out needing to buy it.

"Thank you Izzy" She said grinning up at me.

"Your welcome but we need to go. I promised the Cullens that I would continue to reunite once I had returned" I explained grabbing her hand and tugging her to where I could feel all the Cullens. I knocked on the door and heard the conversation cease. I heard footsteps lead up to the door before it opened in front of us.

"Hello Bella, come on we were waiting for your arrival" Carlisle said in greeting. I smiled and gestured Alice to enter first before following after.

"Hello Cullens" I greeted as I glanced around the room. I saw Carlisle had joined Esme on a love seat. Rosalie and Emmett were sitting on the couch next to an available seat, Jasper and Ashley were sharing a bean bag. Edward was in the corner of the room sitting on the floor in fetal position occasionally glancing at me when he thought I wasn't looking. I sat next to Rosalie and Alice sat on the floor in front of me leaning back onto my legs for back support.

"I'm glad you could join us Bella. I'm sure you have a lot to explain to us and even a few questions for us to answer. We will happily listen and answer when required" Carlisle exclaimed giving me the spotlight. I cleared my throat a little nervous as I stood up avoiding Alice as I did so.

"Um..... It was only a few days ago that you have left but in those few days a lot of things have changed in my life. After Edward had left me in the forest after telling me you were moving I broke down and I felt weak and vulnerable. It was an hour later that I had realised that I was wasting time mourning something that I would never get back and swore to become a better me. A more confident and bubbly person who had a good fashion sense and was fun to be around.

"I had returned to the house and did my usual routine but decided to invite Angela over for a sleep over to go shopping the next day for my new closet. After shopping and becoming best friends with Taylor Swift I discovered I could read minds and was instantly scared of what was happening.

"We had come home to a particular red head in my house. I felt anger boil in my veins as one thing lead to another and I had killed her in front of both Angela and Charlie. They demanded to know what was going on and how I had done that despite me not knowing how I had either. I tried to explain as best as I could without letting them know about you guys and your secret. It wasn't until later that Charlie had proposed a theory of what I could be that it all came clear. I was a witch and I didn't know how or why at the time. It was soon after that, that my mum, Renae showed up for a surprise visit. On that day I found Alice in my room in a bad state and I made a promise to stay by her side and help her through her down. Taylor and Angela visited that day and we had a fun day out and around Forks. It was the the next morning that Alice and I were on our way to school with Angela in the car as well that Alice had a vision of Jane visiting. We decided to pass it off and wait for it to happen that afternoon. As we arrived at school I noticed a certain blonde and her companion waiting for us. She apologised and asked to stay with me as Alice was. I accepted of course and prepared for that afternoon. After the encounter where Jane visited to give us an invitation we were on our way here and now here we are" I finished and let out a sigh before looking around at all the shocked faces that the Cullen clan had. Even Alice as she hadn't heard the full story.

"So that was how you beat the Volturi?" Jasper asked seeming to break out of it first. I nodded in response before taking a seat feeling awkward under their unmoving stares. Alice turned around slightly and grabbed my hand squeezing it in encouragement. I smiled at her in gratitude as she turned back around keeping our hands linked.

"Bella, honey we are so sorry if we knew this was going to happen we would never of left" Esme said looking at me with kind, apologetic eyes.

"It's not your fault Esme, you only followed after your son. Any mother would do that in that situation" I said smiling at her as I saw Edward cringe in the corner. She smiled back happy that I understood and forgave her.

I yawned and my eyes started to droop as I realised how exhausted I was from the day's events.

"I better go get some sleep otherwise I will be very tired tomorrow" I said as I stood up and started to walk to the door with Alice following.

"Night honey have a nice sleep" Esme said appearing in front of me and bringing me into a gentle hug.

"Night Esme" I replied hugging her back.

"Night Belly!" Emmett boomed pulling me into a bear hug whilst spinning around. I laughed at the big goofy teddy bear.

"Goodnight Big brother bear" I replied making him grin.

"Sleep well Sis" Rosalie said taking me out of her husbands arms and hugging me gently before kissing me softly on the cheek and pulling away.

"Have a nice rest Bella" Carlisle said pulling me into a fatherly hug before letting go.

"Night Iz" Jasper said as he hugged me gently before pulling away.

"Night Bella" Ashley hugged me then gently pulled back and smiled. I smiled back before turning my attention back to the rest of the Cullen's.

"Night Bella" I heard Edward whisper from the corner pain apparent in his strained voice. I felt a pang of guilt shoot through my heart before quickly shaking it off. I gave Edward a nod before addressing the others.

"Bye everyone see you all tomorrow" I said my final farewell before pulling Alice out the door and back to our room.

That night I slept fantastically, nightmare and trouble free and I knew why...

****

There's is chapter 23 for you readers! Hope you liked it! Made a long one to make up for the wait!

Vote,Comment,Follow &Suggest

XOXO Meg

Chapter 24 Stories and Preparations

Here's chapter 24 guys! Thanks for supporting me through this book. I know it is very slow and tedious but if I had more time I would update a lot more often. So I take what I can get and try to get inspiration for my lovely readers. Anyway enjoy!

Disclaimer: I do not own twilight or any songs featured in this chapter.

Chapter 24- Stories and Preparations

I woke up and was immediately struck with inspiration for a song. I clicked my fingers as my song book and a pen appeared in hand. I started writing down the lyrics appearing in my head.

I still fall on my face sometimesAnd I, Can't colour inside the linesCause,I'm perfectly incomplete I'm still working on my Masterpiece

And I,Wanna hang with the greatestGot a way to go,But it's worth the waitNo,You haven't seen the best of meI'm still working on my Masterpiece

I finished writing the rest of the song and smiled at my finished product. I quickly got dressed in a blue crop top and ripped jeans adding a few accessories and doing my make up in record speed. Once I was done I grabbed my song book and sped to the music room that I had found when I was wondering around the castle. I sat on the bench of the piano and played around with a few notes.

An hour later I had finished and had a symphony to go with the song. I decided to test out the finished product in full.

"So much pressureWhy so loud?If you don't like my soundYou can turn it down

I got a roadAnd I walk it alone

Uphill battleI look good when I climbI'm ferocious, precociousI get braggadocios

I'm not gonna stopI like the view from the top (Yeah)

You talk that blah blah, that la la, that rah rah shitAnd I'm so done, I'm so over itSometimes I mess up, I f*$% up, I hit and missBut I'm okay, I'm cool with it

I still fall on my face sometimesAnd I can't colour inside the lines'Cause I'm perfectly incompleteI'm still working on my masterpieceAnd I, I wanna hang with the greatsGot a way to go, but it's worth the waitNo, you haven't seen the best of meI'm still working on my masterpiece

Oooh, ooohOooh, aaahOooh, ooohOooh, aaah

Those who mind don't matterThose who matter, don't mindIf you don't catch what I'm throwingThen I'll leave you behind

Gone in a flashAnd I ain't living like that

They talk that blah blah, that la la, that rah rah shitRoll with the punches, and take the hitsSometimes I mess up, I f*$% up, I swing and missBut it's okay, I'm cool with it

I still fall on my face sometimesAnd I can't colour inside the lines'Cause I'm perfectly incompleteI'm still working on my masterpieceAnd I, I wanna hang with the greatsGot a way to go, but it's worth the waitNo, you haven't seen the best of meI'm still working on my masterpiece

Oooh, ooohOooh, aaahOooh, ooohOooh, aaah

I still fall on my face sometimesAnd I can't colour inside the lines'Cause I'm perfectly incompleteI'm still working on my masterpieceMasterpiece, masterpiece (Yeeah)

I still fall on my face sometimes (still fall)And I can't colour inside the lines (inside the lines)'Cause I'm perfectly incomplete (perfectly incomplete)I'm still working on my masterpiece (on my masterpiece)And I, I wanna hang with the greats (oh, with the greats)Got a way to go, but it's worth the wait, no (wait, no)You haven't seen the best of me (b-b-best of me)I'm still working on my masterpiece (I'm still working on my masterpiece)

Oooh, oooh (Yeeah)Oooh, aaah (Hey)Oooh, oooh (Still working on, still working on)Oooh, aaah (Still working on my masterpiece)"

I finished the last note on the piano and sighed. I opened the book to my other unfinished song and worked on finding music for it for the next hour. As I finished writing down the last note I placed it in front of me getting ready to test it out.

"You wanna play, you wanna stay, you wanna have it allYou started messing with my head until I hit a wallMaybe I should've known, maybe I should've knownThat you would walk, you would walk out the door, hey!

Said we were done, then met someone and rubbed it in my faceCut to the part, she broke your heart, and then she ran awayI guess you should've known, I guess you should've knownThat I would talk, I would talk

But even if the stars and moon collideI never want you back into my lifeYou can take your words and all your liesOh oh oh I really don't careEven if the stars and moon collideI never want you back into my lifeYou can take your words and all your liesOh oh oh I really don't careOh oh oh I really don't care

I can't believe I ever stayed up writing songs about youYou don't deserve to know the way I used to think about youOh no not anymore, oh no not anymoreYou had your shot, had your shot, but you let go

Now if we meet out on the street I won't be running scaredI'll walk right up to you and put one finger in the airAnd make you understand, and make you understandYou had your chance, had your chance

But even if the stars and moon collideI never want you back into my lifeYou can take your words and all your liesOh oh oh I really don't careEven if the stars and moon collideI never want you back into my lifeYou can take your words and all your liesOh oh oh I really don't careOh oh oh I really don't care

[Cher Lloyd]Yeah, listen upHey, hey, never look back,Dumb struck boy, ego intactLook boy, why you so madSecond guessin', but should've hit thatHey Demi, you picked the wrong loverShould've picked that one, he's cuter than the otherI just wanna laugh, cause you're tryna be a hipsterKick him to the curb, take a Polaroid picture

But even if the stars and moon collideI never want you back into my lifeYou can take your words and all your liesOh oh oh I really don't careEven if the stars and moon collideI never want you back into my lifeYou can take your words and all your liesOh oh oh I really don't careOh oh oh I really don't care"

I finished the song as I heard movement at the door.

"That was beautiful, I haven't heard that song before. Did you write it?" I heard his voice ask as he moved towards me slowly.

"Yes about a boy that I stupidly fell in love with only for him to leave me all alone in the big bad world. Sound familiar?" I asked him sarcastically. I heard him sigh as he sat next to me on the bench I went to stand up only for him to grab my wrist gently.

"Please don't, can I just explain my actions to you. I won't ask for your forgiveness, just for five or ten minutes of your time and your listening skills" He pleaded pained. I felt a pain go through my chest at his pained expression before I sighed and slowly sat down.

"Make it quick" I said sharply trying to not let him show how him being in pain was affecting me.

"Thank you, I'll start from when I left you" He whispered relieved that I was giving him a chance to explain himself.

"When I left you in that forest Bella I died inside. The further I ran away from you the more pain I felt. I felt like I was empty inside like I had nothing to live for. I had forced my family out of town to protect you from the evil in the world hoping and praying that you would live a happy life after our departure.

" I hoped that you would get married and have kids and grow old like you were supposed to. I didn't want to be the one to keep you away from that happiness. I knew I was being selfish for wanting to keep you and have you forever and it was the hardest thing in my hundred years of life to walk away from you.

"I know that the way that I left you was inexcusable but lying about not caring about you was the only way that I would get you to let me go and you would move on with your life.

"After we left our whole family fell apart. Alice wasn't herself she didn't shop or draw designs she was void of emotions and she spent a lot of time cursing me in her mind for taking her away from her sister. Esme was grieving losing another child. Carlisle took residents in the hospital taking every shift he could to distract himself from his family's and his own misery. Emmett never said a joke or laughed when one of us did something embarrassing. Jasper was in a constant state of self loathing blaming himself for our departure and his family's misery. Rosalie although we all thought that she didn't care about you seemed to be distraught and constantly tried to threaten me in her mind trying to make me return to you or allow them to see you. I never came out of my room, I found that every time that I saw the miserable faces of my family it brought back happy memories of our time together which sent me deeper into my depressed state and I even considered leaving on many occasions but my loyalty to Carlisle and my other coven members stopped me. All of them hated me for what I did and I knew it would take a long time to mend our family back together.

"When we saw you again for the first time everything just seemed to come in to focus again and everything just clicked. It was then that I realise no matter how much I want to protect you from myself, I can not stand to leave you alone again. I love you Bella and I could never survive without you when I left, I left my heart with you. I swear on my life that I will never, ever leave you again unless you order me to" He vowed as he stared into my eyes with complete sincerity.

"It will take time to completely rebuild my trust but I'm willing to take another chance on you Edward. Don't make me regret it" I said as I stood up and grabbed his hand.

"Let's go, Aro wants me" I said to him. When the words finally registered in his head I felt him hug me tightly and swing me around in circles as he dry sobbed into my shoulder. I felt a few tears stream down my cheeks knowing that I would not regret my choice and Edward would make good of his vow.

"Thank you" He whispered as he placed me back on my feet "You won't regret it"

I smiled at him before tugging him towards the thrown room and wiping away my tears. We sped to the throne room and entered to find all the Cullens and Renae hanging up decorations and setting up tables and chairs.

"Aro, I believe you called for me. What is it that you need master?" I asked smiling as he kissed my hand and hugged me as I release Edwards hand.

"Yes I was hoping you could help finish decorating we only have a few hours left before the ball and I thought that you could help get it done in time so we can have more time to clean our selfs up for the ball" He said grinning down at me. I nodded and turned towards the area before turning back to my master.

"What did you have in mind?" I asked as I entered his thoughts and saw what he wanted to be done. I turned towards the partially empty room in front of me and closed my eyes bringing forth the image that Aro shared and willed it to become real. I opened my eyes a little while later and saw that I had accomplished what was asked. I smiled at Aro before curtsying as he kissed my hand in gratitude.

"Is there anything else master?" I asked Aro grinning.

"No that is it Bella dear, go and get ready for the ball. Make sure to save each of your masters a dance" he smiled before stepping back and nodding signaling I was at leisure.

"Come Edward, we should get ready" I said as I walked out of the Throne Room and sped to my room and let him in before following in after.

"Bella? Why is Edward here?" Alice came through the door just before I closed it.

"He apologised and explained his actions and I gave him another chance which he has swore not to muck up" I explained as I hugged the small pixie. She raised her eyebrow at me but questioned me no further, trusting my judgement.

"Sister, I'm sorry from tearing you away from your best friend, your sister. Is there anyway that you can forgive me for my mistake?" Edward said in remorse.

"If Bella has forgiven you for what you did then I guess it is only fair that I give you another chance to redeem yourself but I swear on my parents grave, God or whatever else that if you hurt her even in the slightest you will have one angry pixie on your case and consider that your death sentence signed brother" Alice vowed before smiling and skipping off into the closet to retrieve our dresses.

"Well that went well" I giggled and I saw Edward smile before coming over and wrapping his arms around my waist.

"Well miss Swan, I decided that it was only right to fix my mistakes and try to regain control of my life again so I can prove to this very important girl in my life that I am here to stay unless she orders me away. I just hope in time that she can regain her trust and we can love and cherish each other again forever" He smiled as he looked at me with pure love and adoration. I felt butterflies reside in my stomach as he kissed my nose before slowly releasing me from his grip as Alice walked back into the room. I smiled at Edward and winked before walking over to Alice as she laid out all different make up and hair appliances on a vanity.

"Well unless you wanna stay for Bella Barbie time, I think it's time for you to leave Edward" I smiled as I opened the door as he walked out I shut the door behind us and kissed his cheek before pulling back and going back inside as a crooked grin took place on Edwards face making my heart skip a beat.

"I'll see you soon love" He whispered before walking towards his room to get ready I smiled as I closed the door and sat at the bench in front of Alice.

"Do what you wish Alice" I exclaimed as she grinned before starting on my make up.

****

Here is chapter 24 for you lovely readers! The songs in this chapter are; Masterpiece- Jessie J &Really Don't Care- Demi Lovato ft. Cher Lloyd

Be sure to look them up as both songs are amazing.

Vote,Comment,Fan &Suggest

XOXO Meg

Chapter 25 The Ball

Hey guys here is chapter 25! Hope you like it!

Disclaimer: I do not own twilight or any of the songs featured in this chapter.

Chapter 25- The Ball

As Alice did my hair and make up I decided I would take this time to write down the lyrics running through my head. I snapped my fingers making my song book and a pen appear in my hand. I started to scribble down the song and hummed to myself. I'd occasionally feel Alice peek over my shoulder to read what I had got so far.

Everybody wants what I got with you,Cause I'm standing on top with a killer view,Inspired,Feeling like a million,I'm one in a million,I'm one in a million,million,million....

(Cher Lloyd- With Ur Love)

I kept writing and finished just as Alice put the last finishes on my hair and make-up.

"There, your perfect. Go put your dress on while I get ready" She instruct-ed. I smiled as I unzipped my dress from the bag and stripped from my jeans and crop top replacing it with my gown.

I strut to the mirror and gasped at my reflection. My gown hugged my curves and my smooth legs could be seen through the two splits in the long skirt. My bust was revealed slightly by the v design at the front. I smiled satisfied by my appearance.

"Thank you Alice" I said kissing her cheek as she applied mascara. She giggled and shook her head slightly. I sat on the bed as I placed my heels on and put on my accessories. I put my phone in my new purse along with some money and my credit card.

"I'm ready, you wanna head down the doors are open" Alice said as she put on her heels. Once she stood up I gasped and assessed her appearance.

"You look beautiful pixie" I said as I smiled at her. She grinned back before curtsying.

"Why, thank you" she replied before giggling. She grabbed her purse before exiting and holding the door open for me. I pranced out with a grin on my face.

"Bella! Honey, You look beautiful!" I turned to see my mum walking to us.

"Mum!" I said happily as I wrapped my arms around her.

"Where have you been mum? I haven't seen you much over the past few days" I asked as I pulled away from the hug.

"I've been out exploring, looking at all the tourist destinations and so on. What about you hon?" She asked in return.

"I've been training, catching up with the Cullens and singing. You look very pretty though" I complimented as I glanced over her appearance.

"Thank you" she replied as we started to walk to the throne room again.

"Race you?" I asked as I got bored of walking. Renee grinned whilst Alice shook her head wildly.

"Nah-uh not when I did your hair like that! It will get wrecked!" Alice whined as she gave me pleading eyes.

"Fine can I at least teleport us their. Hair intact" I pleaded. She rolled her eyes before taking my hand and nodding.

"Meet ya there mum" I said before we appeared in front of the throne room doors. A second later Renee appeared next to me still grinning.

"I won" I whispered to her before the doors opened.

I strut in and smiled at the vampires inside looking curiously to see who entered.

"She's human" I heard one of them whisper.

"Bella dear, nice of you to join us" Aro appeared hugging me and kissing my cheek.

"Master Aro, I wouldn't want to be anywhere else" I grinned at him.

"Everyone this is Isabella Swan, a new member of our coven" Aro introduced me to the confused vampires.

"Call me Bella" I laughed as I saw that they were still confused by my 'human' state.

"Bella here, is our new weapon" Aro said grinning down at me. I rolled my eyes at my master playfully. I heard a few snickers go around the room, probably vampires wondering how a 'human' could help the Volturi in any way.

I nervously clicked my fingers as the pressure of everyone in the room staring got to me, fire appeared on the tips of my thumb and middle finger. As I let that fade I made a small tornado with my index finger swirling my finger around and around, I concentrated on watching it to distract me. I could see Aro looking around and laughing silently at the shocked faces of the vampires at my little nervous tricks which I stopped since I realised it was gaining me more attention .

"Bella here is a witch" Aro said causing me to look up smiling shyly.

"Master may I be dismissed to go and catch up with some guest" I requested as the shocked stares didn't drop.

"Sure Bella Dear, make sure to save your masters a dance and say hello to Marcus and Caius if you see them" I nodded before using my powers to find the Cullens in the crowd I grabbed Alice and Renee's hands before teleporting to them. I could here the shocked gasps at my sudden disappearance and heard Aro laugh as he made his way back to his throne. I laughed silently as a few vampires noticed me and their eyes widened further.

"Greeting Cullens!" I said as I walked to them grinning when they all turned in my direction.

"Bella dear you look wonderful" Esme exclaimed in awe. I smiled at her as she pulled me into a gentle hug.

"Thank you Esme, You look beautiful" I complimented her long lilac colored dress.

"Thank you dear" she replied pulling away with a gentle and warm smile.

"Hey there little sis! How ya been Belly?" Emmett greeted hugging me tightly. I laughed as I hugged him back.

"Be careful of the hair Emmett!" Alice warned a second later her eyes glazed over.

"DON'T YOU DARE!" Alice screeched pointing an accusing finger at Emmett who immediately dropped me and held up one hand over my hair intimidatingly. Before he could do something I teleported from under his hand to in front of Rosalie.

"Bella!" Rosalie exclaimed surprised before hugging me being cautious of my hair.

"Hey sis" I replied pulling back. I turned to Carlisle curtsying as he kissed my hand before pulling me into a fatherly hug.

"Good evening Carlisle" I greeted as we pulled back.

"Indeed Bella, you look beautiful" He complimented me smiling.

"You don't look to bad yourself" I replied grinning. He bowed mockingly.

"Why thank you" He replied before laughing as everyone joined in.

"How are you darlin'?" Jasper asked in his southern drawl. I turned to him and hugged him.

"Fantastic, what about you?" I asked in return as I pulled away.

"Never better" He replied smiling.

"Ashley" I greeted as I pulled her into a soft hug.

"Bella" she smiled as she pulled back.

"Hello Love" Edward greeted wrapping his arms around my waist. I turned in his arms facing him. He smiled as he glanced over my face with love.

"Edward" I greeted before kissing his cheek. I pulled away keeping his hand around my waist as my grin widened. I turned to the Cullen's and my mother's shocked faces realizing they didn't know.

"Um... Edward and I talked and I've gave him another chance" I explained. I was engulfed in a huge family hug all of them having huge smiles upon their faces. As everyone pulled away I looked up at Edward to see him smiling admiringly at me. I returned it before he quickly pecked the tip of my nose.

"Bella" My mother came up beside me finally speaking up.

"Oh... Mum, This is the Cullen's. Introduce yourself guys!" I encouraged smiling as I wrapped my arms around Edwards waist smiling at him. He smiled crookedly back before we both looked back at the group.

"I'm Carlisle and this is my wife Esme" Carlisle said shaking Renae's hand. Esme stepped forward enveloping Renae in a gentle hug.

"Nice to meet the mother of such a wonderful person" Esme said as she pulled away and smiled at me in a motherly way.

"I'm Alice as you already know" Alice giggled.

"I'm Rosalie and this is my husband Emmett as you know already" Rosalie smiled warmly while Emmett saluted mockingly.

"I'm Jasper and this is my mate Ashley" Jasper stepped forward shaking her hand and Ashley hugged Renae gently.

"And I'm Edward, as you already know" Edward smiled at my mother not moving from my side.

"Yes I know about you Edward. I swear if you hurt my daughter again, you will have one angry witch on your case. So don't muck this chance up and we will have no problems" Renae smiled innocently at the end. I burst out laughing at my mother causing everyone else to laugh even Edward and Renae.

"Sorry, just had to get the protective mother out. But it's nice to see you again Edward" She said smiling.

*******************************Hope you enjoyed it!

GO CHECK OUT MY OTHER STORY!!! MESSAGE ME IF YOU WANNA TAKE OVER WRITING IT!!!

Vote,Comment,Suggest &Fan

Chapter 26 Dance the Night Away

Hey guys here's chapter 26! Hope you love it!

Disclaimer: I do not own twilight or any songs featured in this chapter.

Chapter 26- Dancing the Night Away

"May I cut in?" A voice asked behind Edward. I saw master Caius standing there smiling politely.

"Sure" Edward replied before kissing my forehead and going to dance with Alice.

"So enjoying the Ball so far?" Caius questioned as we started to move gracefully around the room.

"Yes, I am very much" I replied smiling "what about you master Caius?"

"I'm enjoying myself, it's better then our normal nights here" He answered smiling. We continued on gliding around the room in silence just enjoying our time.

"May I step in Brother?" I heard Marcus's gruff voice ask.

"I will see you soon Bella" Caius smiled before making his way back to his throne.

"Bella, You look beautiful tonight. What a lovely dress" He complimented as we glided around the dance floor avoiding colliding into other dancers.

"Thank you, Master. You look pretty good yourself" I replied smiling. As I looked over his classic black and white tux.

"Thank you, have you gotten the chance to eat yet. We had a meal put aside especially for you" He said smiling. I grinned at how thoughtful that was.

"Thank you Master, I will be sure to stop by when I get hungry" I replied in gratitude. He smiled as we continued to dance in silence.

"May I?" I heard Aro ask Marcus.

"Why, Of course Brother" Marcus answered before walking back up to his throne.

"Dearest Bella, You look wonderful! Have you enjoyed your time in the castle so far?" He asked as we moved around the dance floor.

"Thank you Master, I have enjoyed my stay very much" I replied as I grinned.

"That is pleasant to here, promise you will visit whenever you can" He said as we continued to dance and he spun me around.

"Any chance I get" I vowed as I smiled "If you need me I am a phone call away"

"Thank you dear Isabella" He exclaimed as a smile came upon his face.

"Anytime Master Aro" I said.

"I'm getting kinda hungry, care to escort me to my awaiting meal" I giggled as we stopped dancing.

"Why, I'd be delighted" Master Aro chuckled lightly as we linked hands and he escorted me off of the dance floor and through a door into a room which held a large table and multiple chairs. No one was inside as I took a seat in one of the chairs.

"Felix, Bella's meal please" He requested. Felix walked out through doors that looked like it lead to a kitchen.

"Here you go Bella" He said as he placed it in front of me. I looked and saw that the plate held lamb chops, mash potato, boiled vegetables and gravy in a small pot on the side.

"Thank you, it looks wonderful" I said as my stomach growled. They both chuckled.

"Let's leave the poor girl to eat" Aro chucked as Felix left and he followed.

I started to eat right away and finished in record timing. I grinned as I walked through the kitchens doors and quickly placed the dish down on the nearest bench before going back out. I walked up to the bar that was serving out blood to all the vampires and sat on one of the stools.

I waited to be served patiently as I looked around watching all the vampires interact with each other.

"What can I get for you?" I heard a voice ask. I turned and smiled politely at the bar tender.

"Do you happen to have any soft drink?" I asked. He look surprised for a second before nodding.

"I have Coke, Lemonade, Fanta and Lift" He replied.

"Could I please get a Coke and also some mountain lion for a friend" I requested he nodded and grabbed the drinks. It was an open bar so as soon as I had the drinks I headed towards where I found Edward sitting alone at a side table looking at all the Vampires.

"I got you a drink" I appeared behind him. He smiled as I handed him his drink and took a seat across from him.

"Mountain Lion" He grinned after he had taken a whiff " my favourite"

"I remembered" I said as I giggled.I took a sip out of my cup and the fizz of the coke made me smile.

"Where have you been?!" Alice exclaimed as she plopped down next to me "I was looking for you"

"I was eating" I replied casually.

"Come on! I have planned something for you! Bella, Edward come on!" She yelled excited. She dragged me from my chair and I looked back at Edward curiously, he shook his head smiling not giving away what alice was talking about. She continued to drag me through the crowd until we reached the front. She pointed towards the corner where I could see Jane setting up a microphone near a guitar stand.

"I thought you could sing for everyone. I had Edward make up some background music for that song you worked on before. I may have stolen your song book but I promise I put it back" She said in one big rush. I raised an eyebrow before smiling at the small pixie.

"Fine" I gave in. I turned to Edward who was smiling crookedly.

"You really spent your time making up music for this song for me" I said as I looked at him admiringly. He nodded before kissing my cheek and dragging me on stage.

"Just sing when you here the cue in the music" He said before letting go of my hand as I stood in front of the microphone. He took a seat and strummed the guitar checking it was in tune before plugging it into the amplifier. He smiled at me as I started to get a bit nervous.

'You got this' Alice mouthed at me when I looked at her.

'Thanks' I mouthed back before deciding to get every bodies attention.

"Good evening everyone, I'm Bella and I will be singing an original song of mine called 'With Ur Love'" I spoke gaining the attention of everyone in the room. Edward started to strum and as soon as I felt the time come I started to sing along.

"Da da da da dum dum da dum dumDa da da da dum dum da dum dumDa da da da dum dum da dum dumDa da da da dum dum

Baby, you the best 'cause you worked me outI keep building walls up but you tear 'em downI'm fighting, I don't wanna like it but you know I like itBut you know I like it Used to always think I was bullet proofBut you got an AK and you're blowing throughExplosive, you don't even know it, I want you to know itI want you to know it

All of them other boys can walk awayThey ain't even in the game'Cause they know that you own itYou got this swag, you got this attitudeWanna hear you say my name'Cause you got me...

Flying with your love, shining with your love, riding with your love.I feel like I'm on top of the world with your love.One hit with your love. Can't quit with your love. So sick but so what?I feel like I'm on top of the world with your love.

Everybody wants what I got with you'Cause I'm standing on top with a killer viewInspired feeling like a million, I'm one in a millionI'm one in a millionI ain't even here, I'm in outer spaceLike I'm Venus, you're Mars in the Milky WayIt's crazy what you're doing to me, how you do it to me.

How you do it to me, to meAll of them other boys can walk awayThey ain't even in the gameYou got this swag, you got this attitudeWanna hear you say my name'Cause you got me...

Flying with your love, shining with your love, riding with your love.I feel like I'm on top of the world with your love.One hit with your love. Can't quit with your love. So sick but so what?I feel like I'm on top of the world with your love.

Da da da da dum dum da dum dumDa da da da dum dum da dum dumDa da da da dum dum da dum dumDa da da da dum dum"

I finished and grinned as I hugged Edward. Everyone clapped and I heard who I assumed to be Emmett wolf whistle causing me to laugh along with Edward. We walked off and went over towards the back corner. Everyone went back to what they were previously doing as soon as we walked away.

"I love it, how could you put it together so fast?" I asked amazed at how good the background music fit the song.

"I knew it would mean a lot to a very special girl that I love" He replied.

"Where is this lucky girl and how come I've never seen her" I asked jokingly.

"Well she is kinda mysterious. She has the most beautiful brown hair that has curls that bounce when she walks" He grabbed a small bit of hair that was hanging loose and twirled it around his finger twice before dropping it back to it's place "She has the most beautiful chestnut brown eyes that light up a whole room" He placed both his hands on my cheeks and ran his thumbs underneath my eyes "She has the most amazing and adorable laugh that makes you want to laugh with her" I smiled before giggling shyly making him chuckle " A body that seems it was meant to fit perfectly with mine" He wrapped his hands around my waist and pulled me closer "And the most kissable tender red lips that give the most passionate and loving kisses" He whispered.

"Well, now I have to meet this girl" I whispered as he leaned in.

"She's a bit busy right now, she's about to share a kiss with the one she loves" He replied before smashing his lips on mine. I wrapped my hands around his neck running my hands through his hair. He groaned as I pulled myself tighter to him. We both pulled away slightly breathless as we both had our eyes closed and foreheads touching. He pecked my lips one more time before resting his head on top of mine as I nuzzled into his neck.

"Isn't she a lucky girl" I said against his neck as I laughed lightly. He chuckled along and kissed the top of my head.

"I think he's the lucky one" He replied as he pulled back slightly and kissed my cheek.

"Bella, I love you" Edward whispered as he stared into my eyes showing pure love and admiration. I grinned and didn't even hesitate as I replied.

"I love you too, Edward" I whispered back before sharing another passionate kiss. And continued to dance the night away and just enjoy the time together.

*************************************There is chapter 26! Hope you like it! Love it? Hate it? Tell me in your comments!

Vote,Comment,Fan & Suggest

XOXO Meg

Chapter 28 High Expectations

H ey guys!

Sorry that it has been so long since I have updated. Had a big move and another almost move overseas. Also lots of school as year 11 is challenging. Haven't had very good internet. Few family problems. Plus the time that I have to write I struggle to think of what to write. Anyway enough excuses and I will start writing.

****

I woke up in my bed as the sun started to rise over the land casting sun rays directly into the room. They hit my back creating warmth and waking my body up. I opened my eyes as a smile formed on my face. I looked out the huge windows and gazed at the beautiful view. I sat up as a yawn escaped my mouth and went to stand up when a hand grabbed mine. In an instant I had the person telepathically pinned against the wall over the other side of the room.

"Bella" Edward whispered pained as he struggled to breathe. I gasped and released him immediately speeding over to him.

"I am so sorry. I forgot you were here" I checked him over after he had landed back on his feet. He stroked my cheek and moved a piece of my hair behind my ear hushing me.

"It is okay love. It was just self defence" He responded with a chuckle. He wrapped his arms around my waist and pulled me closer to him immediately bringing a smile to my face. He kissed my nose then leaned down to whisper in my ear.

"You look beautiful in the morning love" He stated in a hushed voice. I shook my head as he placed a singular kiss on my neck making my heart beat faster.

"Bella!" Alice came barging out of our closet.

"Yes Alice?" I responded as I spun to face her fully.

"I thought we could go shopping today before we leave tomorrow. It is Rose' s Birthday after all. Maybe see a few tourist attractions as well?" Alice asked hopefully as she made a pouty face.

"Umm.... I guess we can do that but-" I was cut off by Alice as she bounced.

"Yay!" She exclaimed and bounced up and down.

"BUT I want to be back before 4pm so I can spend some time in the training room before we leave" I stated as I held up a finger in Alice's direction.

"Deal" Alice agreed smiling. Rosalie emerged from the closet and I chuckled a little.

"Is there anyone else in our closet that I should know about Alice?" I asked as I chuckled.

I watched as Esme walked out showing Alice a shirt she had found. I laughed as Alice and everyone else but Esme did.

"What is it?" Esme asked as she looked around confused.

"Oh, nothing. Just there are so many people in my wardrobe" I stated as I walked into the closet to take a seat on the couch in the middle.

"So what are you girls doing in our wardrobe at..." I checked my phone "7am in the morning"

"Planning our outfits of course" Alice stated as she pranced around the closet pulling out different clothes.

"Happy Birthday by the way Rose. How old are you this year?" I asked with a smile.

"I don't even want to say it aloud. It makes me sound so... old" She said it as she chuckled. I watched as Alice was still looking around and she was starting to get stressed.

"Alice. Imagine your outfit" I commanded and watched as Alice stopped what she was doing and closed her eyes for effect. Rosalie and Esme watched on in curiousity.

I entered Alice's mind before snapping my fingers and she was wearing it. Alice opened her eyes and smiled at her ensemble.

"You are a life saver" She stated as she twirled infront of the mirror. She inspected the black flowy dress in admiration and twisted her feet as she examined the black heeled boots. "Thanks Bell"

"My turn. Please" Rosalie begged with a smile on her face that was full of excitement. I nodded and she closed her eyes. I entered her mind and saw the outfit but also was able to see an image of a little boy running around in a front yard. I was confused by the image but did not ask further as that was Rose's business. I created the outfit with a snap of my finger and rose jumped in excitement.

She wore black jeans, a white tank flowy blouse and black and red Christian Louboutin heels. She looked perfect, like a model straight from the front cover of vogue.

I turned to Esme and nodded as she soon closed her eyes like her daughters had. I entered her mind and saw the outfit she desired and with the click of my fingers it was on her. She wore a nice flowing purple dress that came to the thigh with ruffles on the top and a belt at the waist, this paired with nice purple ballet flats.

I turned to Rose as my curiousity got the best of me. I entered her mind again and tried to forward my thoughts into her head.

In head;B: Hey Rose. It is Bella. Is it okay with you if I enter your head to have this conversation with you?

R: Of course Sis. What do you need?

B: When I entered your head before I saw a vision of a little boy running through a backyard. I don't mean to pry and you don't need to tell me, but I was curious of who he is?

R: Oh.... That is what I imagine Emmett and I's kid to look like... if it were possible for us to have a kid

B: I am sorry for your pain...

R: It is okay... It is not your fault. This is who I was destined to become. I obviously wasn't meant to have a child and although it hurts I have come to terms with it.

B: I love you Rose

"Love you too Sis" Rosalie said aloud as she hugged me. I could tell she was a little upset by what we were discussing but she gave me a small smile as she pulled away.

I put a hand on her stomach and stared at it intently. She looked at me confused but did not move as she trusted my actions. I focused all my energy on her womb and I acted on instinct as I moved my other hand also to her stomach. Alice and Esme watched on as they were giving me strange looks. I yet again looked to Rosalie and saw as a look of realisation covered her face bringing on a sense of hope.

I tried harder hoping with enough magic I could follow through with my intentions.

I contacted my Mother through thought asking her for her help immediately. I was hoping that I could do this for Rose and Emmett. I felt that they deserved such a gift.My mother appeared in my room and sped to the wardrobe.

"You called?" She said with a smile.

"Yes, I need your help" I stated as I gestured to my hands over Rosalie's stomach.

In head;Bella to Renae: I want to give her a baby boy or girl. She deserves it.

R: What a wonderful idea. We can try. Let's hope we can do it together.

We both placed our hands over Rose's stomach and slowly we brought her womb to life. We made her able to cary a baby. We made her more human like. Focussing we planted a fertilised egg inside her newly reformed reproductive organs.

"Rosalie, you are now a pregnant vampire/ human hybrid" I stated as tears brimmed my eyes at the joy that adorned her face. She started to dry sob in happiness as she took me into a tight hug.

"I will never be able to repay you for what you have done today. Thank you so much Bella and Renae. You have got me the most wonderful gift anyone could ever ask for" She whispered as she hugged Renae.

"Happy Birthday Sis" I said as I hugged her again.

******************************Like it? Love it? Hate it? Needs Improving?

Tell me what you think in the comments below.

Like,Comment,Fan &Keep Reading

XOXO Meg

Chapter 29 Shopping

We walked down the main streets of Volterra, admiring the old shops and restaurants adorning the cobbled streets. I walked with my hand linked with Rosalie and Alice who was linked with Esme. We had a collection of bags piling up on our arms and it wasn't going to stop growing for the next hour or two.

"Alice, can we stop to feed the human. I need breakfast" I asked with a smile as she nodded and dragged everyone into a café. I quickly ordered and ate so as not to interfere with an anxious Alice's schedule any further. I did feel a little bit bad though when Alice paid double for the order to be done faster and put in front of others orders.

We were soon wondering the streets again with Alice dragging us into many shops, especially the designer ones that looked way too expensive.

****

"Ahhhhhh" I whispered as I sat down and took off my heels, flopping down onto my bed back at the castle. I heard a knock on the door not a moment after. I sighed before heaving myself up again and heading towards the door. I opened it to see a beaming Emmett standing at my doorway.

"I am going to be a father!" He boomed before taking me into his giant arms and swinging me around laughing in happiness. I laughed with him and wrapped my arms around him in return "I am going to be a dad! You have no idea how much this means to me Bells! I owe you the world!"

"You deserve it Brother Bear" I state as he places me back on my feet with an ear splitting smile on his face.

"I love you Bellerina" He said before walking away happily towards his room. I swear I even saw him skip a little causing me to smile and giggle at his goofiness, he will be an amazing father.

"I love you too Em" I whispered after him knowing he will hear me.

****

"Without the physical shield this time" Aro commanded as he was testing my limits.I nodded and put my thumbs up indicating I was ready.

The entire guard rushed towards me for the third time today. I put up both hands and immediately paralysed all of them.

"Okay back to the start. Only your physical and mental shield this time" Aro commanded again as he sat down on the spectators bench. The Cullen's and a few other guest that were still in the castle were watching as well. I nodded again and put my thumb up.

I placed a physical shield around me in a bubble, my mental shield already in place. The guards ran at me again and hit an invisible wall all at the same time making some of them fall to the floor. I wrapped a physical shield in a bubble around all of them. Making them levitate above the ground in the invisible bubble.

"I can shrink this so everyone inside turns to ash. I win" I explain before safely placing the guard back on the ground.

"Well done, Isabella. You truly are remarkable. One of a kind, isn't she brothers?" He gloated in glee. "We are so happy to have you as a part of the gaurd"

"Thank you Aro, if I am no longer needed can I be dismissed to go and pack?" I asked politely.

"Certainly, be sure to come and say goodbye before you leave" He requested.

"Of course" I replied before teleporting me and Alice to our room.

"I don't want to leave yet" Alice pouted.

"Me either, but we have to. We can teleport back whenever we want" I state with a smile. She smiles back and hugs me.

"I love you Iz" She whispers into my shoulder.

"I love you too Ally" I reply before a knock interrupts our hug. I break away and open the door to see a girl there with blonde hair and gold eyes.

"Hi, you don't know me but I saw what you did back there and I need your help" The girl says as she glances over her shoulder down the hallway in nervousness. "Can we talk somewhere safer? It is important"

I nod hesitantly before teleporting her, Alice and I into the woods in Forks. She looked around and nodded before walking a little bit closer.

"I need to show you something. I need you to enter my head to understand" She requests. I nodded entering into her thoughts and watching as a child's face comes to her head. She a supernatural beauty about her.

"This is Tatia. She is a vampire/human hybrid. I am her biological mother. I gave birth to her as a human, her father being a vampire. I nearly died giving birth to her but her father saved me. Tatia and our coven are about to be accused of creating an immortal child. In which we will be punished by death even though the child was beared by human flesh. We need help to prove to the Volturi that we have not committed a crime, no fighting, no killing. We have very little time the accuser is on a plane as we speak. Will you help us?" She pleaded.

"I need to see her for myself. I promise not to harm her, I would just like proof" I state as I take her hand in my left and Alice's in my right.

"Imagine where you would like to go" I instruct. I read her thoughts and teleport in front of the house she imagined.

"I am Jasmine by the way and this is the house of the Boltanic coven" She introduces herself and gestures to the wood cabin. We are in a highly wooded forrest. Looks like Canada maybe.

"Tatia! We have more guest for you to meet" Jasmine yelled towards the house. A young 7 year old girl skipped gracefully down the stairs towards us.

"Mama. Will they help us?" She asked Jasmine in an innocent voice.

"They have come to see you and then they will decide" Jasmine explained.

"Hello Tatia, I am Bella and this is Alice it is nice to meet you" I exclaimed as I held out my hand for her to grasp in her cute little hand and shake.

I could see the flush in her cheeks and the bright green emerald orbs that hypnotised you with every blink. I could also see her paleness and felt the strength she had slightly through her hand shake.

"I believe you, I see the flush of her cheeks and hear her heartbeat but can also feel her strength and her paleness. I will help you protect her. I will start by researching into anyone like her to see how they developed" I state as I watched the child intrigued. "I will stand with you and help you prove your innocence as I can see no crime has been committed here"

"Thank you, your help means so much. The power you hold will help us greatly. We can help you research if you want?" She offered as she showed her gratitude towards our help.

"Oh no, that won't be necessary. You continue to collect witnesses. Here is my phone number" I handed her a card "call me with details and updates. I will do my research and will tell you what I hear on the Volturi's side. I give you my word that I will protect Tatia"

"You have no idea how much this means. I will be forever in your debt" Jasmine exclaimed with a broad smile shaking my hand again.

"It is what is right" I state before nodding my head and stepping away from them.

"I will see you soon. Jasmine. Tatia" I nodded at them both before teleporting Alice and I back to the castle.

"Well that was interesting" Alice finally spoke up.

"I know. Now how are we going to research this in such a short amount of time?" I asked her.

"I may know a person"

****

Chapter 30 Doing What Is Right

H ey guys here is another chapter! Enjoy!

****

"Goodbye Aro, I will see you soon" I said as he gave me a kiss on the cheek before I picked up my bag and linked hands with Edward and Alice. I teleported us to the place Alice had imagined and smiled as I looked beside me to Alice. I had teleported our bags to the Cullen's place.

"What now?" I asked her. The Cullen's had flown back to Forks whilst we came here to search for the person Alice believes can help "Actually, first, where are we?"

"We are in a forrest in Thailand" Alice states before stepping forward and cupping her hands around her mouth and hollering a unique series of sounds. I heard the pattering of footsteps following soon after.

"Alice? Is that really you?" A female voice whispered before embracing the pixie in her long slender arms. The women was tall, lean and tan. She was wearing weaved palm leaves as a skirt and a bra.

"It has been a long time Masia" Alice stated with a smile as she pulled away from the embrace.

"You can say that again" The women, Masia replied with a smile "What is it you have travelled so far for. Are you in trouble?"

"We need your knowledge. I have heard some whispers about some vampire tribes in this area and was curious if any of those whispers happened to involve a human/vampire hybrid?" Alice asked in a careful way as if not trying to anger her.

"And if I have?" She asked cautiously back.

"We need help to prove a girl's innocence, a child just like that hybrid. The Volturi believe that they are immortal children or could be like immortal children and we need proof that they are not harmful and can live alongside the humans in peace. If you know of someone who is like this child it could help us greatly with no harm to the child" Alice explained, pleading with Masia.

"How do I know this isn't a trap?" She questioned slightly suspicious.

"I vow to you that this is not a trap" Alice stated with full sincerity. I used my powers to wash away the feeling of suspiciousness and made her feel she can trust us.

"Hazel!" She called loudly which was followed closely by the pitter patter of footsteps again.

"You called Masia?" The woman asked politely. I looked closer at the woman and saw the slight flush of her cheeks and could hear her fast heartbeat, but she was also very pale and was too fast to be human.

"Meet my friend Alice and her friends..." Masia trailed off realising she didn't know our names.

"I am Bella and this is Edward" I introduced "It is nice to meet you Masia and Hazel"

"What can I help with?" She asked.

"We need your help to prove a child's innocence. She is a hybrid like you. You will not need to fight, we just want to prove that your kind are not harmful" I stepped forward to explain.

"Are you sure she will not be harmed? How can you be sure?" Masia questioned.

"I am a witch and I have gone against the Volturi in my practice time. I know that I can stop all of them if needed. Would you like me to show you?" I responded.

"How can you show us?" Hazel was curious.

"Can I enter your head?" I asked permission. They looked to each other and hesitantly nodded.

I showed them an image of the Volturi guard all paralysed, one of them tied to the ground and an image of them all levitating in my physical shield.

"Is this real?" Masia asked Alice.

I encircled them in a bubble and made them levitate off the ground. They looked shocked as they stared at their feet then at me.

"We believe you and we will help" Masia stated looking to Hazel who nodded.

****

We stood as a group in a large clearing in the Canadian forest. I had Alice by one side and Edward by the other. Behind us was Masia and Hazel who had travelled with us yesterday. It was a day before the Volturi were meant to arrive. I had warned the group that the whole clan was arriving and that they expected me to meet with them here. I felt as though I were betraying them already but I knew what was right. I would go over to their side to make Aro feel comforted but I would explain that I had gotten here earlier and had already assessed that Tatia was no harm to our secret. I knew it would be risky to be on the other side but I knew if a fight were to break out I could protect both of the groups from killing each other.

"Bella, if you could join me to discuss your plan with our friends" Jasmine requested.

"I will be the peacemaker of this battle. I have an alliance to both sides and wish that a battle will not occur. Tommorow I will be standing with the Volturi. I think that is the side that will give me the best shot to stop a fight. If Aro believes that I am loyal to his side than he will be more likely to listen to what I have to say. If a battle does occur however I will stop either side by paralyzing each of you until everyone calms down enough to continue the discussion and make peace. Just know that I will protect you and I will try my hardest to have this confrontation have a peaceful solution" I explain to the group.

"How do we know you are telling the truth?" A blonde haired woman asked.

"What do I need to do for you to trust me?" I queried back.

"They stay on our side" She stated as she pointed at Alice and Edward. I looked at both of them to see if they agreed and they nodded.

"Okay"

Chapter 31 Peace or War?

Hey guys here is chapter 31! Enjoy!

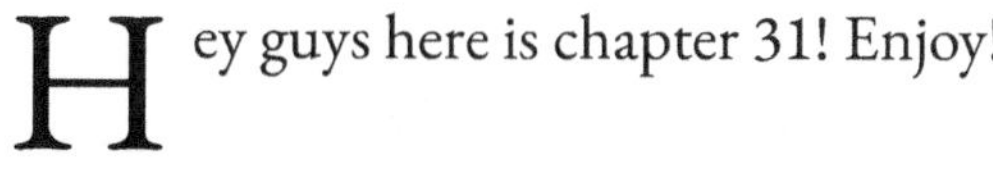

****

"I love you Edward" I state as we stand in a group waiting for the Volturi. He pulled me by the waist into his arm and put his cold forehead against mine.

"I love you too" He replied "we will get through this"

"I know" I whisper with a smile before I bring him in for a passionate kiss. I pull away and hug Alice before kissing her cheek.

"Love you Bells" Alice stated. I hug her one more time.

"Love you too" I reply with a grin.

"I think you need a more superior outfit" She smirks.

"What do you have in mind?" I questioned as I entered her head before making myself wear it.

"Nice" I complement as I look at myself through her mind.

I walked over to Tatia and gave her a hug. Over these few days we had become really close as I am teaching her how to expand her physical shield. She is so sweet and amazing, Jasmine is very lucky to have her as a kid.

"If something happens to me, you know what to do. Remember, it is like an elastic band. If worse comes to worst, place it around the Volturi and then shrink it. I believe in you" I smiled at her. She hugged me and I swung her around in circles.

"Thank you Bell Bell" Tatia says as she gave me a kiss on the cheek.

"If we get through this I will make sure I visit regularly" I promise as we interlock pinky fingers.

"Thank you so much for your help Bella" Jasmine says in gratitude.

"It is what is right. I will protect Tatia at all cost and if I fail than I know that I have taught her to protect herself and the ones around her. So I have hope she will make it through this. You have a wonderful daughter, you should be proud" I reply with a grin. She pulls me into a short hug before going over to join Tatia and her mate.

I walk over to the other side of the field and turn to face the group. I blew a kiss to Edward before I heard the synchronised steps coming towards the opening. I felt the gaurd join me with the masters at my side. Aro gave me a sweet kiss on the cheek before turning and assessing the opposition.

"Alice. Edward. What are you doing on the law breakers side?" Aro asked as he gave me a confused side glance.

"We do not want the child to be harmed" Alice replied as she grabbed Tatia's hand.

"Are you so naive to support an immortal child?" Aro mocked as he gave a small evil smirk "even after what happened to the Denali's mother?"

Alice sneered in reply to Aro bring up that story.

"She is not immortal" I state. Aro tilts his head towards me.

"Go on my dear Bella" he encouraged.

"She is half human, half vampire" Jasmine spoke up.

"Don't be ridiculous she is clearly an immortal child. We are not blind" Caius exclaimed on the other side of me. Aro held up his hand to silence Caius and directed his focus to Jasmine.

"And you are?" Aro questioned.

"I am her biological mother, Jasmine, and this is my mate, Nate. I concieved Tatia when I was still human and I was transformed after the birth. She has blood flowing through her veins. Can you see the pink in her cheeks. Can you hear her heart beating?" Jasmine continued on. Aro took a few steps forward and hushed the gaurd. His face lifted in surprise.

"What does she eat?" He pressed.

"She can survive on both human food and blood" Nate spoke for the first time.

"Brother she is still a threat to us all. We don't know of her kind or what she could be capable of" Caius frowned. I gave him a bewildered look to which he replied with a glare.

"I don't like what you are suggesting Caius. I do not believe this child should be killed. I think she has a better chance at keeping our secret than many other vampires roaming the world today. She is innocent. No crime has been committed here and I think we should leave this poor family alone" I glared back at Caius.

"How do we know for sure that she is no harm?" Caius pressed and stepped towards me threateningly. I glared at him and gave him a warning look that told him if he came any closer I would destroy him. Edward growled and Caius reluctantly stood down.

"Stop..." Aro commanded towards us. He turned towards Jasmine "I want to meet her"

He started to walk towards the center and I followed him as he requested. Jasmine, Nate and Tatia walked forward. I gave them a reassuring look. Aro offered his hand to Tatia and with a nod from me Tatia took his hand. I had warned her about his gift earlier and she was prepared. I manipulated what Aro was seeing so it looked like I arrived just a few minutes before them and had never met Tatia before.

"It is true" Aro exclaimed in wonder "I have never heard of anything like this before!"

"Brother" Caius warned.

"I know that she could still possibly be a threat... It will be a hard decision" Aro stated as he rubbed his chin thoughtfully "If only there was a way we could be sure that this child won't be a threat to our kind"

"What if there was? Would that make you believe that she will not threaten our secret? Would you leave us alone?" Jasmine asked.

"Obviously. But it is impossible to be sure" Caius claimed.

"Hazel" Jasmine called and at the speed of light Hazel was standing beside Jasmine in the middle of the field. Hazel held out her hand to Aro for him to read. Once again I manipulated what Aro could see and made him believe that Jasmine had met her in the forest and taken her back here.

"Remarkable" Aro exclaimed.

"I am Hazel and like the child I am a half human, half vampire hybrid. I have been living nearly 200 years and in that time I have never threatened your kind. In my time I have met others like me. All of us have kept your secret, all of us are not a threat. We are just like you but with human qualities. We grow at a fast rate until we stop growing as soon as we turn 18. I live with a tribe in one of the many forrest of Thailand and we feed on animals, just like Tatia and her family. Our kind are no threat. I am proof of that" Hazel finishes her speech. I give her a beaming smile.

"I think we are done here" Aro exclaims.

"You can't be serious?!" Caius yells in fustration.

"Do you not trust me brother?" Aro retorts back with a menacing smirk.

Caius glares and growls before turning and stomping off. The rest of the gaurd soon followed and in the blink of an eye they were all gone.

"I am sorry for any inconvenience this has caused you. Consider it an unfortunate misunderstanding" he nodded apologetically towards the group. He offered me his arm "Bella?"

"I will politely decline. I think I will stay and talk to them a bit longer and find out more about them. I am very intrigued" I smiled at my master.

"Suit yourself. Make sure you visit us soon but for now, keep yourself safe" he requested before kissing my cheek and speeding off in the direction of the Volturi. There was a huge cheer as he left.

"We did it!"

Chapter 32 It's All About The Competition

H ey readers! Here is another chapter! Enjoy!

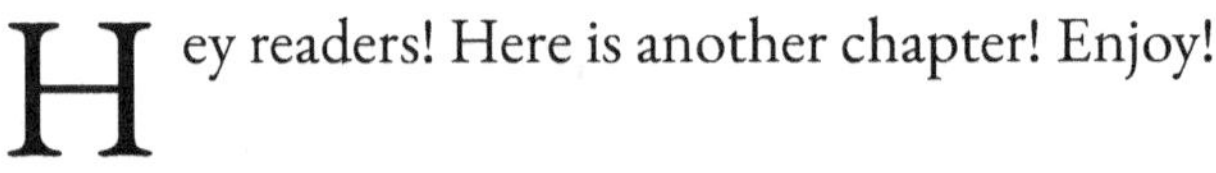

"Izzy!" Angela screamed as she embraced me tightly as soon as I got through the gate at Seattle Airport.

"Ange!" I exclaimed, just as excitedly. I pulled away and gave Charlie a hug.

"How was the holiday?" Charlie asked with a smile. He hugged Alice.

"It was amazing! Italy is the prettiest place in the world! The people there were super nice too" I replied.

"And don't forget the shopping!" Alice bounced with a smile.

"Typical Alice" Charlie joked as he ruffled her hair. I felt an arm wrap around my waist and turned to smile at Edward. Charlie noticed his presence and his face immediately turned sour.

"What is this Bella?" Charlie asked as you could hear the malice in his voice. He was glaring intently at Edward.

"Well Edward surprised us in Italy and we kinda... he kinda... I may have accepted his request to... Um... be his girlfriend again?" I answered as I watched Charlie's face turn more and more red.

"We will deal with this later" Charlie stated as he fumed. He looked around to make sure he hadn't caused a scene and started to stalk towards the door. Alice, Angela, Edward and I followed after, giving each other numerous side glances.

'I am so dead' I mouthed to Alice. Who nodded and mouthed back '6 feet under'.

Edward was rubbing soothing circles on my hand as we walked side by side out the door towards the police cruiser waiting in the parking lot.

"Bella. In the front" Charlie commanded in a choppy voice.

"Dad if Renae has accepted this I think you will have to as well. I love Edward and he loves me. He had to move with his family, he had no choice. He dumped me so that he wouldn't hurt me as we all know long distance relationships are very hard" I lied to Charlie. He looked at me still unconvinced "Yes he hurt me, your little girl but if I have forgiven him and given him a second chance than you should too. Please Dad"

"How will you maintain the distance?" Charlie still remained uptight.

"We will be moving back. Our family didn't enjoy being away from our home and away from Bella" Alice answered for me. I beamed in Charlie's direction, a smile he hadn't seen in weeks.

"Fine. One last chance. But don't think I won't shoot you if you hurt her again" Charlie threatened and I snickered at his threat. I imagined the bullet just rebounding off of Edward's cold hard skin or me stooping it mid air "What?"

"Nothing. Just imagining that situation in my head" at that remark, Edward and Alice let out a beautifully chimed laugh from the back seat.

"And why may I ask is that a funny situation?"

"You know that secret that I can't tell you. It is an inside joke" I try to word in a way so as not to give too much away. Charlie raised his eyebrows but did not question any further.

"I think you should tell them Bella. They can be trusted" Alice smiled.

"Are you sure?" Alice nods. Charlie becomes immediately intrigued and Angela perks up.

"Well promise not to freak out and let us explain before you do. Actually it might be best if you pull over for this dad" I suggested. Charlie does so but with a worried look, with his eyebrows furrowed.

"The Cullen's are Vampires" I state and watch as Charlie is shocked which quickly turns to panic "Wait before you assume anything they survive off of animal blood, they do not harm humans. They also have super speed, super hearing, enhanced eyesight, super strength, pale skin, they are immortal and they shine bright like a diamond in the sunlight. Many have special gifts like Alice can see the future, Jasper is an empath and Edward can read minds. The other Cullen's do not have any powers"

"So your a witch and they are vampires. What else exists werewolves? Fairies?" Charlie asked in bewilderment, trying to let it sink in.

"Werewolves? Yes. Fairies? Not that I am aware of" Alice answered him.

"Wow this is a lot to take in" he exclaimed.

"Are you okay Angela?" I asked as I turned to see her reaction.

"You won't hurt me will you?" Angela asked both of them.

"You can trust them Angela. They won't hurt you in the slightest, they wouldn't hurt a soul" I answered for them. They nodded in agreement with complete sincerity on their faces.

"Well than I don't care what you are. You can't help what you are and considering you are using it for good by not harming humans I respect that" Angela stated with a smile and a nod. Alice squealed and hugged her. Angela laughed and hugged back.

"Wait... Carlisle is a doctor?" Charlie queried.

"Carlisle has been alive for a few decades and has mastered his self control. Since he survives on animal blood, he has no desire to hurt humans. In fact his vampire abilities significantly help him in completing his job" I explain.

"So you are dating a vampire and you are totally okay with it?" Charlie asked with a bit of concern.

"Well, he is dating a witch that could kill him any second. If he is okay with it, I am too" I state with a smile in Edward's direction.

"You better not hurt her buddy. I wasn't joking when I say I will shoot you... with wooden bullets of course" Charlie threatens.

"Myth. Wood does nothing to a vampire. The only way they can be killed is if you rip them apart and burn them, which is impossible for any human to do" Alice informs.

"Well I will find a way to hurt you" Charlie glared at Edward through the mirror.

"Do like... Sleep in coffins?"

"Myth" Alice stated.

"Moat? Castle?"

"Myth and also myth" Edward chimed in.

"Mmmm... bats?"

"Myth" I state.

"Do all vampires have gold eye?" Angela asked.

"No. Vampires that survive on human blood have red eyes" Alice informs.

"The werewolves? Where are they found? Do they change on the full moon? Oh god... do I know any?" Charlie questioned.

"There are some in the La Push area. As for you knowing any... I am not sure" Edward replied.

"Can you tell? I mean if they are a you know" Charlie asked concerned.

"No, not unless they tell you but many are tall, tan and they have a circular tribal tattoo on their shoulder" Alice explained.

"Jacob?!" Charlie exclaimed in shock "I knew there was something wrong with him as soon as he got a haircut and started to hang out with that group of boys. Do they.... do they kill people?" Charlie asked. It looked like he didn't really want to know the answer.

"No, in fact they try to stop people from getting killed. They hunt us, they are one of the few supernaturals that can kill us, along with Bella of course. We have a treaty with the tribe at La Push as we drink animal blood, so they do not harm us" Edward explained.

"Wow" Charlie whispered.

"Are you okay dad?" I asked to make sure he won't have a heart attack.

"I will be fine, it is just a lot to take in" He stated as the car was then engulfed in a few minutes of dead silence. Charlie pulls out, to start the journey back to Forks again. The whole way he seemed to be deep in thought. The car remained silent until Alice started a conversation with Angela. I felt a hand tap my side and noticed Edward had stuck his hand between the seat and the door. I grabbed it and smiled to myself as we continued driving.

After a few minutes I got bored of the drive and decided to test my teleportation skills. I clicked my fingers and all of a sudden all of us, including the car, were inside the carport attached to our house. Charlie and Angela were shocked whilst Edward and Alice shook their heads in amusement.

"It was taking too long" I shrugged.

"Maybe warn the humans next time. Try to avoid nearly giving us a heart attack next time" Charlie stated with an eyebrow raise.

"Sorry dad" I apologise with a sincere smile. He nodded and got out of the car with the rest of us following soon after.

****

"We need to start preparing for the competition tomorrow night" Angela stated as we were eating dinner, well apart from Edward and Alice of course.

"May I ask what competition?" Edward questioned.

"Bella here is in a singing contest tomorrow at 5" Angela explained for me. I nodded along as Edward looked shocked at first than happy.

"I will make sure I am there. I will tell the rest of the family tonight, I am sure they will come and support you too" Edward beamed proudly. I blushed looking down.

"Have you got an outfit?" Alice bounced.

"Yeah, Taylor helped pick it out" I saw her face drop so I immediately tried to cheer her up "but I will need someone to do my hair and make up?"

"Yay!" She exclaimed bouncing again. Charlie chuckled at her behaviour and smiled.

"With me by your side you will look like an angel tomorrow night! Eek!"

Chapter 33 All In This Together

Hey readers! Here is another chapter! Hope you enjoy!

****

Beep. Beep.

I was parked outside the Cullen's house waiting for them to come out for school. I had teleported here so I could get here early enough to not be late for school. Alice and Edward came out the door with Esme and Carlisle following them. I teleported in front of them and gave them a big hug.

"Have a good day at school dear" Esme wished me luck as I got in my car.

"Nice car" Edward compliments before getting in the passenger seat with Alice in the back.

"Thanks, she is my baby" I reply as I rub her leather seat before taking off down the driveway again. The drive to school was short and silent. I held Edward's hand the whole way and just listened to the radio.

As soon as we arrived at school, everyone yet again stared at the car. As Alice and Edward emerged, their faces turned to shock. Edward opened my door for me and immediately offered me his hand. He pulled me out of the car and into his arms. He planted a sweet kiss on my forehead before he grabbed my waist in one hand and started walking towards the office to reclaim his old schedule.

"Wait here" he requests before going in to deal with the paperwork and grab his timetable.

"What are they doing back?" Mike was all of a sudden in my face.

"They moved back because Carlisle liked the job here. Why are you so concerned?" I asked as my eyebrows furrowed. I had gotten good a lying for the Cullen's, although I didn't like doing it.

"You aren't seriously going to forgive him that easily are you?" Mike questioned. He made it sound like it was a ridiculous thing to do.

"I love him Mike. He had no choice when he moved away and he dumped me to protect me from the distance. In fact he pushed his family to return here, where they are happy. Now please stop with the questions. I am with Edward and I hope it stays that way until I die" I reply with an annoyed grimace. I felt Edward come up and wrap his arm around my waist.

"Is there a problem?" Edward queried as he saw the look on my face and most likely heard the entire conversation.

"No, Mike was just leaving" I state with a pointed glare. Mike gave me one last shake of his head before walking off into the buildings of Forks High School.

"Still have that crush on you?"

"Unfortunately" I replied with a frown. Edward rubbed my back in soothing circles before leading me to our first class.

****

I heard the seat next to me scrape against the floor and looked up. I was currently in the cafeteria eating lunch with Alice, Edward and Angela. The person sat down and smiled at the group.

"Hello. What is your name?" I asked in a welcoming tone. The girl had brown straight hair at shoulder length with bangs and was wearing sunglasses. She moved the glasses down to her nose.

"Guess who?"

"Tay?" I asked "is that you?"

"Mmmhmm" she replied. I got up and hugged her excitedly. Angela came and joined along with Alice.

"You made it" I state in happiness.

"I didn't wanna miss you getting a record deal" she exclaimed confidently.

"What if I don't?"

"Whether you get the deal or not you are coming to be my opening act on tour anyway. Then if you haven't already got the deal you definetly will by the end" She offered. I smiled widely and hugged Taylor tightly. I felt tears of happiness fall from my eyes.

"Please tell me those are happy tears"

"They are" I replied.

"As your manager I would advise you take this deal" Angela smiled widely.

"I would love to be your opening act on tour on one condition"

"Name it"

"You have to sing one duet with me in the concert" I suggested.

"Easy done" Taylor smiled and pulled me under her arm "we will get you famous in no time"

"I can't wait to have fans! To be able to do something I love and be paid for it because of their support... is amazing!" I state excitedly.

"You'll be a great pop star" Taylor complimented.

"Where have you travelled from to get here?" Angela asked.

"Home, I am on my break from my tour in America. In a 3 months I perform in Asia then Australia and New Zealand then over to the UK, Europe and finishing with some islands around the world, mostly to relax a little and give a few performances" she explained. "So you will be freshly graduated and ready to take on the world, it can be a working gap year"

"I can't wait"

****

"And done. Your perfect" Alice stated. We were currently sitting in the dressing room back stage in the gym where the contest was being held. As I was waiting for Alice I had been practicing the piano keys me and Edward went through earlier in my head and drumming my fingers against the table much to Alice's annoyance. I could have done this with magic but Alice insisted that she do it by hand.

"Can I open my eyes now?"

"Go ahead" Alice encouraged. I opened them to come face to face with a mirror. My hair was perfectly curled with the front strand clipped back with an elegant pin. I examined the pin to see the Cullen's crest laying on it with diamonds on either side leading up to it.

"Welcome to the family" Alice exclaimed with a beaming smile. I got up and pulled her into a tight hug.

"Thank you. This means so much"

"We all decided it was about time" She pulled away "now continue admiring my hard work"

I looked back into the mirror and saw my make up was beautiful. The dress that Alice convinced me to wear instead of my other one hung gorgeously. My heels were high and were just over my knee. Overall I looked gorgeous.

"Thank you Alice. You made me look amazing"

"You already looked amazing, I just enhanced the beautiful basis" Alice complimented "Okay you are on in 1 hour. Go warm up and there is a piano in the back room which you can use and not be heard from the gym. I will be in the audience. I love you and good luck! You will be great, I know it"

****

□ABDCBB□

The piano keys made sound with the pressure of my fingers. I was in the back room warming up my voice like Taylor had taught me to.

"□D, d, d, d, d, d, d□. □ G, g, g, g, g, g, g □. P, p, p, p, p, p, p □. Me, me, me, me, me, me, me □. □We, we, we, we, we, we, we□. □Ta, ta, ta, ta, ta, ta, ta □" I continued to warm up.

"Yeah-ey-eh... yeah-ey-eh...   yeah-ey-ayee... yeah-ey-ayee... yeah-ey-y eah-ey-yeah... yeah-ey-yeah-ey-yeah" I did my voice variations. I decided to use Little Mix's song, different beat to do my last bit of warm ups.

https://www.youtube.com/watch?v=SSU7SPLzvNg

"Your on in 15" A crew member told me as they quickly bustled past the door. I decided to run through my song one last time before going to wait in the curtains.

****

I did some nerve breathing techniques as I waited for the act before me to finish. He was attempting a magic act but by the looks of it the audience was not very interested in his tricks. I felt sorry for him although he was pulling out the old and boring tricks. When he bowed the nerves really kicked in. A piano was moved on stage and the lights were off. I walked over in the dark and sat on the piano bench. I took a deep breath and started to play the opening notes. The lights faded on and it was just me and the music.

https://www.youtube.com/watch?v=KX-Foo3Mqz8

I sang like my life depended on it. I held the high notes as long as I could and truly tested my voice. I had chosen this song to really try to showcase my potential. I played the ending notes and the lights faded.

It was completely silent for a few seconds and as I got up to walk off there was suddenly a huge uproar of applause. I beamed and walked off stage.

****

Chapter 34 This Is Happening

Enjoy this chapter as it is the very last one!

****

"Just sign here" The scout gave me a contract as soon as I walked out from behind stage. I beamed and jumped up and down. I grabbed the extended paper and began to read the conditions.

"I only have one problem. Can I have my own manager?" I queried as I glanced at Angela.

"We don't usually allow that but... if they get qualified.... sure" I screeched in joy before giving the contract to Angela to check over and after a while of reading she gave it back with a nod.

With a stroke of a pen I was officially signed with universal studios.

****

A few weeks later

****

"My baby girl is all grown up" Renae stated with a frown as she adjusted my gown and hat.

"Mum I will visit at least once every year, I promise" I vowed. A tear slipped out of her eye followed by a whole Dam. I hugged her and rubbed her back.

"I got VIP tickets for you and Dad to go see one of Taylor's concerts in London and I will book the flights closer to the date so you will be able to see me then"

"I am so proud of you! I am sorry I couldn't come to the performance but the video you sent was amazing! Any way I love you and I should probably go and sit down" Renae kissed my forehead farewell.

"I love you too mum"

****

"Bella Swan"

I walked up the stairs to collect my certificate with a huge smile. My heels clicked as I approached the principle. He shook my hand and presented me with the certificate. We posed for the camera and smiled as we received applause. I blushed when I heard Charlie whistle loudly.

"Congratulations Bella. You have earned this" the principal complimented.

"Thank you" I reply with a smile and nod before walking off the stage.

****

"Now for a performance from our very own, Bella Swan"

I walked on stage and stood infront of the microphone.

"Here is to us" I direct to all the graduating students.

[There should be a GIF or video here. Update the app now to see it.]

Once I had finished I bowed and reapproached the microphone.

"Life may be hard but you can reach your dreams if you give your best. We are the future and we have the potential to be whatever we want to be. We just have to believe... so believe in me my fellow graduates, as I believe in all of you" I blew a kiss and waved as the applause followed me off stage.

I would miss Forks High, I had grown accustomed to this school... I learnt to love this school and I would now have to leave it all behind to chase my dream.

But it is worth it to do the thing I love.

****

"You are all ready to go" Alice stated as she closed my bag. Today was the day I left for Asia. I would meet up with Taylor over there and work through the concert plans with her over a month before the concerts actually started "did we forget anything"

"If worst comes to worst I will just use magic to get whatever I am missing. The question is are you, Angela and Edward ready?" I asked. I found an excuse to bring these three with me as Angela was my manager, Edward was my instrumental coach and Alice was hair, make up and my personal designer.

"We are all packed and ready to go" she replied with a beaming smile as she bounced up and down excitedly.

"Well then let's go"

****

"Goodbye Esme. I will miss you. Make sure to come and see me when you can, I can get you tickets" I offer as I hug her tightly.

"I love you Bella, you are like a daughter to me. Stay safe" she kissed my forehead and let me continue on down the line.

"I will see you soon Carlisle. Thank you for coming back and allowing me to have my own personal and favourite doctor back in town" I joked "I will miss you"

"I will miss my favourite and most accidental prone patient as well. Stay safe and if you need me I am a phone call and snap of the fingers away" He made a witch joke that made me laugh.

"Bye Sis. I might come down under to watch you sing" Rosalie offered with a hug.

"I would love that"

"Bye bye Bellaroo" Emmett pulled me into a hug and swung me around "and thank you for granting me the best thing in the world, fatherhood"

"I will miss you brother bear. If anything happens with the baby, call me. Oh and I want to be there for the birth too!"

"Goodbye darling" Jasper drawled in his southern accent. I hugged him.

"See you soon Jasper"

"Goodbye Bella" Ashley farewelled as she hugged me before letting me go to say my final goodbye.

"I will miss you Dad" I turn to Charlie who looked very sad "I will make sure I teleport over for dinner at least once a fortnight"

"You would really do that?" He asked hopefully.

"Of course"

"I will miss you Bells. Stay safe" he demanded as he hugged me fiercely.

"I love you Dad"

"I love you too Bells"

I pulled away and wiped away a stray tear. I would miss this lot dearly but it is what I have to sacrifice to achieve my dream.

I am on my way along a new and unknown path. Do I know where it will lead me? Who knows?

All I know is I will get there someday...

*********************************The End....